NAHANNI
RIVER OF GOLD...
RIVER OF DREAMS

NAHANNI
RIVER OF GOLD . . . RIVER OF DREAMS

Canadian Cataloguing in Publication Data
Hartling, R. Neil, 1961-
Nahanni: River of Gold, River of Dreams
Includes bibliographical references and index.
ISBN 1-895465-06-0
1. South Nahanni River (N.W.T.) – Description and travel. 2. Canoes and canoeing – Northwest Territories – South Nahanni River – Guidebooks. I. Canadian Recreational Canoeing Association. II. Title.

FC4164.N3H37 1993   917.19'3   C93-090098-7
F1100.S6H37 1993   73804

Published By...
The Canadian Recreational Canoeing Association
1029 Hyde Park Road, Suite 5
Hyde Park, Ontario, Canada N0M 1Z0

Photo Credits...
Photographs not credited within the book have been taken by R. Neil Hartling.

Printed and Designed By...
Port aux Prints Ltée.

Printed on
Recycled Paper

Please Note...

This book is a narrative, not a guide book. The author, publisher, and associated contributors assume no responsibility for injury or loss that may result from practical implementation of the information found within.

Nahanni River Adventures and the Canadian Recreational Canoeing Association advocate the wearing of personal flotation devices (lifejackets) when canoeing, particularly on northern mountain rivers.

FORWARD

I have canoed in Canada and in many other parts of the world. As my years so rapidly passed by, my hope to paddle in the Northwest Territories and Yukon seemed somewhat out of reach. Accordingly, I have a deep sense of gratitude to Neil Hartling who made it possible for me to experience both the Nahanni and Yukon Rivers. Paddling in the North reminds me of what it is to be Canadian and what inspires me to live in Canada.

Neil's book is a compendium of reflection and ideas for wilderness travel. Readers, now and in the future will benefit from his sensitive insight of the Nahanni region.

For many years, I worked with students at the University of Toronto in outdoor education. We spoke of travelling unknown paths and reaching for our outer limits. For me, the Nahanni River was the fulfillment of those ideas. Neil has the most admirable trait of gentle leadership in which he and his guides offer an adventurous, yet safe journey. They understand people and attend to building a cohesive group while addressing the aspirations and limitations of each individual.

The components so delightfully included in this book will always be treasured by the many persons who accompany Neil or his guides along the trails of the North. The inclusion of legends, the descriptions of geological phenomena, the sharing of ideas and thoughts, the reporting of history, the inclusion of good humour makes the text an excellent reading experience.

There was gold along to Nahanni to be sure, the gold of the river, the canyons, the sky and all the elements that produced my memorable journey. Yes, I will return to that vast and brooding land and I will travel again with Neil and his dedicated associates.

Kirk Wipper,
President
Canadian Recreational Caneoing Association
Founder, Kanawa International Museum of Canoes and Kayaks*

(renamed Canadian Canoe Museum which includes the Kanawa International collection)

HAPPY NAHANNI DREAMS!

Neil

1993

To Judy and the guides

INTRODUCTION

To this day the Nahanni remains an isolated region. Most of the mountains are nameless, and those that have names support the region's mysterious reputation. Deadmen Valley, Headless Creek, Funeral Range, Burial Range, Hell's Gate—all speak of a land of myth, mystery, and romance. It is a country where clouds drifting below the mountain tops and canyon rims redefine the relationships among earth, sky, and water.

Ever since reading Dick Turner's book *Nahanni* as a teenager, I have been a hopeless topophiliac with an incurable love of this place. Enmeshed in my relationship with the Nahanni country are the personalities of characters attached to the Nahanni. Its legends and lore are inseparable from its physical features. I predict that you too will fall in love with the regal river with the beautiful name.

I have found gold in the Nahanni. Not the shiny, metallic sort, but the kind that lets me review without regret, a decade spent sharing the valleys and canyons of this enchanted land with fellow travellers on the river. These years have been rich. Sharing this land through this book and our trips down the river is my way of giving something back.

I wish you many pleasant Nahanni dreams.

Neil Hartling
Whitehorse, Yukon
January 1993

TABLE OF CONTENTS

ACKNOWLEDGEMENTS

It has been the nature of my work for the past decade to distil details of the south Nahanni River and pass them on as interpretive information to participants in our adventures. This book is based on the resulting "oral tradition" and for this reason the sources of some of my information have become cloudy or lost. Where possible I have followed the conventions for recognition, but I would like to point out here that over the years we have received helpful input from:

Pierre Berton and the Right Honourable Pierre Elliot Trudeau who were very helpful with Chapter 11. I drew upon Mr. Berton's writing extensively for the details of the chapter.

The Canadian Parks Service, specifically the staff and resources of Nahanni National Park. Those who manage the park clearly do so as a labour of love and it is in this spirit that they have shared their knowledge of the region over the years.

The Canadian Parks Service also furnished the original data for the diagrams.

The Department of Mines and Technical Survey, Ottawa, from which the original data was obtained for rendering the topographic maps.

Explore Magazine in which the *"Prospectors story"* of Chapter 4 first appeared.

Peter Jowett, a former Nahanni National Park warden who under contract to us developed a staff interpretive manual. He is currently writing a guide of the region.

Pat and Rosemarie Keough, authors of the *Nahanni Portfolio*, which has been a reference piece on the Nahanni since 1988.

Drs. George W. Scotter and Derek Ford who, under contract to the Canadian Parks Service, made a significant contribution to the pool of environmental and geological knowledge of the Nahanni area. This data has been invaluable to all Nahanni interpreters over the years.

Wendell E. White, author of *The Birth of Nahanni: Nahanni Beguli*, a compilation of historic information Mr. White gathered while serving as a school teacher in Nahanni Butte.

IN ADDITION IS A CAST OF MANY:

Joseph Agnew, Executive Director of the CRCA, without whose assistance this book would not have been.

Peter Bregg for his recollections of the Trudeau Expedition.

The Canadian Recreational Canoeing Association (CRCA), who is always willing to assist paddlers in any way possible.

Fellow guide and friend Randy Clement, a source of encouragement and good humour.

Ric Driediger, who provided the initial invitation to visit the Nahanni.

Mentors Dr. Garry Gibson, Dr. Harvey Scott, Mark Lund, and Mors Kochanski.

The Government of the Northwest Territories – Travel Arctic.

Ted Grant of Simpson Air who has contributed support and enthusiasm over the years.

Patricia Halladay Graphic Design for rendering of the diagrams from the original Canadian Parks Service information.

Judy Hartling, who provides patience and support above and beyond the call.

Roy and Lois Hartling (Dad and Mom), the unsung heroes.

Mr. Gavin Henderson for his accurate recounting of the events leading to the preservation of the park.

Edwin and Sue Lindberg who provided photographs.

Father Pierre Mary OMI, a steadfast friend.

The Mason family for the picture of Bill on Sunblood Mountain.

The Nahanni-Ram Tourism Association.

My colleagues in the Nahanni River Outfitters Association: Barry Beales, Wendy Grater and David Hibbard.

Andy Norwegian who verified the Slavey place names.

Editors: Glenn Rollans, Keith Parkkari, Terice Reimer-Clarke, Lisa Hartling, Roy Hartling, Dr. Lawrence Farries, Rob Prosper, Dick Moore …

Urs and Marianne Schildknecht – Liard Tours, who assisted in getting the outfitting business off the ground.

Mike Stilwell of Sail North and Jacques VanPelt of Subarctic Wilderness Adventures who are partners in our Boreal Woods and Waters Expedition.

Wayne Towris, Ben Gadd and Chris Harris who provided initial publishing advice and Norm Kagan and Lyn Hancock for their enthusiasm.

My friends in Nahanni Butte, Fort Simpson, and Fort Liard, who have provided support, encouragement, and friendship.

The helpful staff of Port Aux Prints Ltée in London, Ontario.

The Canadian Heritage River System

South Nahanni River

The South Nahanni is one of the world's great rivers. It's visitors are treated to a unique blend of scenic grandeur, wilderness adventure and solitude. Tumultuous rapids and meandering calm water have cut deeply into the Mackenzie mountains, creating three towering canyons and Virginia Falls, twice the height of Niagara. Deep caves puncture the walls of First Canyon; Rabbitkettle Hotsprings have built the highest tufa mounds in Canada. In recognition of this unique heritage, the South Nahanni River has been proclaimed a Canadian Heritage River.

– A statement of the Canadian Heritage River Systems.

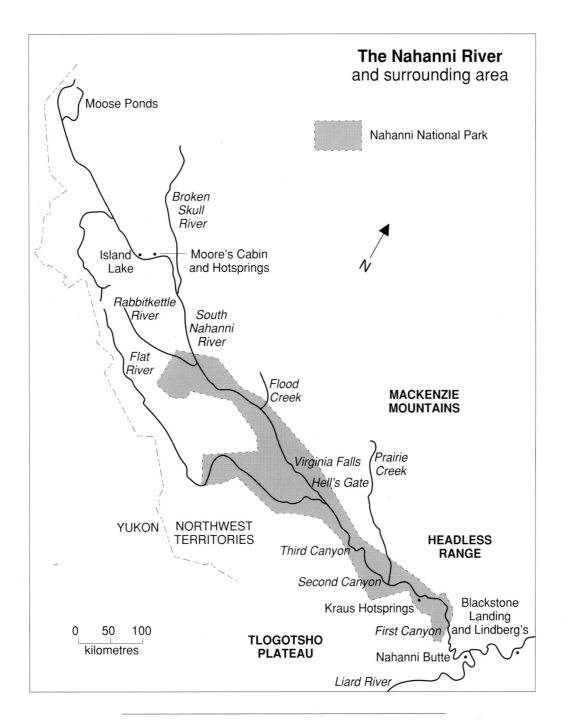

The Nahanni River
and surrounding area

Nahanni National Park

Moose Ponds

*Broken
Skull
River*

Island
Lake — Moore's Cabin
and Hotsprings

N

*Rabbitkettle
River*

*South
Nahanni
River*

*Flat
River*

*Flood
Creek*

**MACKENZIE
MOUNTAINS**

Virginia Falls *Prairie
Creek*

Hell's Gate

YUKON \ NORTHWEST
TERRITORIES

**HEADLESS
RANGE**

Third Canyon

Second Canyon

0   50   100
kilometres

Kraus Hotsprings

Blackstone
Landing
and Lindberg's

First Canyon

**TLOGOTSHO
PLATEAU**

Nahanni Butte

Liard River

Chapter One

NAHANNI BOUND

"So you're going up the Big Nahanni? Boy you've bitten off something this time! They say there's canyons in there thousands of feet deep, and water coming through faster'n hell."

"But people have gotten through, haven't they?"

"Oh, I guess they have just got through—years ago. But canyons—and sheer! Thousands of feet!"

"If people have got through, there must surely be some ledges or something where a man can tie a canoe and camp and sleep?"

"I don't know. There ain't many that have come back to tell about it. Men vanish in that country. There were some prospectors murdered in there not so long ago, and down the river they say it's a damned good country to keep clear of. ..."

Advice Given Raymond Patterson in Fort Smith on his way to the Nahanni in 1927.
— From *The Dangerous River*

"One, two, three, lift ... OK, let's try again and this time tilt the canoe a little more."

This is always an awkward time. Twelve of us, mostly strangers to each other, were attempting to load more than a tonne of gear, canoes, food, and people into the limited interior of a De Havilland Twin Otter aircraft.

The material goods had been carefully calculated to sustain us comfortably for two weeks in the wilderness. But by now, the new members of our group were wondering whether this had ever been done before and who these two yokels were who seemed bent on defying physics by stuffing matter into non-existent space.

Finally, with some choice phrases, some sweat, a budding feeling of camaraderie, and an ambience of "What have I gotten myself into?" the plane was loaded.

Fortunately, enough space remained to fold down the jump seats for the six of us who had waited for the second flight. The other six members and their supplies were waiting for us upriver.

A DEW SHROUDED YELLOW DRYAS. WITHIN A FEW DAYS THEY "UNTWIST" AND BLOOM, COVERING THE GRAVEL BARS WITH FLUFFY BLANKETS.

— D. SALAYKA

OUR BASE AT SIMPSON AIR IN FORT SIMPSON, NORTHWEST TERRITORIES.

The fuel tanks were filled, and the co-pilot gave us the standard aircraft spiel. A high-pitched whine cut the air as the pilot started one engine and then the other.

Aircraft fly when their lift and thrust exceed their drag and weight: a seeming impossibility for this plane. Every square inch of space in the cabin was occupied. I wondered at the ability of the slender landing gear to bear the weight, as we bounced down the gravel strip, until finally we bounced up and didn't come down.

We gained altitude over the flat, lush, Liard plain. Soon it gave way to the Mackenzie Mountains. From where I sat at the back I could imagine the doubts of my fellow travellers. Only this afternoon we had met at the small airport outside Fort Simpson in the Northwest Territories of Canada. They had come from all corners of the globe, and every step of their journey seemed

Leo Norwegian poses with a skin boat which he and a companion built to descend the Flat and Nahanni Rivers in August, 1966.

— *W.D. Addison*

to require that they squeeze into a smaller aircraft. A classic DC3 took them the last leg into Fort Simpson. As I had watched the passengers filing down the ladder I picked out my new companions. The task was easy since they were all dressed in the sort of outdoor clothing that says, "I am about to embark on an expedition." They had identified each other the same way in the Yellowknife airport two hours before. While the baggage was unloaded we were all formally introduced, and I could tell I was being sized up.

Since then, we had been into town, made a last-minute stop at the local store, and arrived at the Simpson Air hanger to wait for the Twin Otter. While we talked about clothing, equipment, the immediate itinerary, and individual expectations, a fly crawled into the ointment.

Murphy's law reigns supreme over wilderness expeditions, so I wasn't surprised when Mansell

Patterson, the operations manager at Simpson Air, informed me that our flight would be set back for several hours while the engineers worked on the aircraft.

"Fine, take all the time you need," I told Mansell. It's false economy to rush aircraft maintenance, especially up here.

The delay proved to be an opportunity. My groups had a standing invitation at the Native Friendship Centre for tea and bannock (traditional baking-soda bread).

Fort Simpson sits on an island in the Mackenzie River and has a population of about 800. It's typical of many northern towns: the economy is based on providing services to residents, government departments, and resource developers. You can walk from stem to stern without difficulty. Our walk to the Friendship Centre took us through the heart of town.

As luck would have it, Leo Norwegian, a local Dene elder (pronounced deh-nay) (and the only person I know to have survived three plane crashes) was teaching a group of school-aged children the nearly forgotten art of building a spruce-bark canoe. His large hands deftly plied the large sheet of spruce bark, peeled earlier that day from a standing tree. Leo had harvested spruce roots from the muskeg and stripped them of their skin to yield a shiny, woody, yellow core for stitching the canoe cover. He had also collected spruce gum to seal the seams.

Our group was entranced as Leo talked while the slender, shallow canoe took shape. The spruce-bark canoe was used for muskrat hunting on lakes and for descending rivers in the spring after travelling upriver on foot during the winter, he told us. Larger boats were made of moose hide stretched over a spruce-pole frame. An entire family and dogs could descend a river in one of these, if they could defend the moose hide from hungry scavenging animals.

The Dene in the Nahanni area speak the Slavey dialect. Leo taught us the word Dehcho, the Slavey name for the Mackenzie River. The Nahanni, he explained, was called Dahʔaa Dehé. Fort Simpson was Łiidlįį Kúé: "community where the two rivers meet."

We returned to Simpson Air with a fresh perspective on the land we were about to enter, a little humbled by the realization that our challenging land of adventure has been home to generations of Natives who relied on little more than their ingenuity and skill to survive. Leo's stories also helped balance the stories of murders, headless men, gold mines, tropical forests and evil spirits that have been told about the Nahanni in the twentieth century, and which—along with the promise of scenic grandeur—drew my group to the North.

Lupine.

— *D. Ladouceur*

Orchid at Virginia Falls.
The Subarctic forest is rich
in plant life such as
Orchids and Lupine.

Chapter Two

Into the Kingdom of Nahendeh

March 1st, 1829
I have made arrangements with Mr. Smith that a new post shall be settled
on the Nahany River, for the convenience of the Nahany Tribe…which will
require an establishment of Six Men besides the Clerk in charge, with an
outfit of Twenty Five pieces Goods, and may be expected to yield,
about 20 to 25 Packs Furs, value about £2000.

A dispatch from George Simpson Esqre., Governor of Rupert's Land, to the
Governor and Committee of the Hudson's Bay Company
— From The Dangerous River

A bit of turbulence brought me back to the present.

Glancing at my watch I saw that it was 10:00 p.m. The evening light rendered the landscape below as a medieval scene of ramparts, moats, canyons, buttresses, and spires. Crammed into the cabin and surrounded by a tightly fitted assortment of packs, food barrels, sundry equipment, and boats, we sat with faces pressed to the windows.

A phenomenon overcomes me each time I experience this flight. As I looked at the panorama unfolding below the wings, I heard an orchestra. The deepest, richest strains of Vivaldi, Pachelbel or Grieg reverberated somewhere between my ears, accompanying the dramatic displays, and serving as a prelude to the adventure ahead. As winged observers, we glided through the peaks, first the Ram Plateau, then Tundra Ridge, the Sombre Mountains, and the Nahanni Plateau.

The twisting form of the Nahanni River appeared below us as we rounded a sharp peak. As we lost altitude, the age of this river became evident: ages older than its mountain guardians. Much of the river was spared from the last ice age because the mountains of the Yukon to the west hold back precipitation. This fact preserved unique geological features—karst landforms, canyons, caves, and mountains—and earned the Nahanni the distinction of being named the first-ever United Nations World Heritage Site. This distinction recognizes the area as part of the heritage of all of humanity. Resembling a prairie river as it meanders, the Nahanni seems a contradiction in this rugged mountain setting.

We were entering Dahʔaa got'ie gondéhé, a name which translates to "the land of the Naha." The Naha were the mountain tribesmen who had inhabited the region and were feared by the Dene. Dahʔaa got'ie gondéhé k'eh deh, the Slavey name for Nahanni, means "river of the land of the Naha." Nahendeh means "our land".

AN AERIAL VIEW OF THIRD
CANYON AND PULPIT ROCK.

— HENRY MADSEN

Cameras were poised at the windows, and already some had said that they wished they had brought more film. A good sign, confirming for me that they were caught by the spell, seduced by the Nahanni, which would make my job all the easier. All I had to do was not interfere with the magic.

Sometimes, at this point in the flight, I interfere with the magic by getting sick. I am one of the unlucky few who can only fly comfortably if I gaze at the distant horizon or consume enough anti-motion-sickness medicine to choke a horse. One time, while flying the same route in a Beaver aircraft, I was sandwiched in the back between two women. I had a large pack on my lap and couldn't see a thing in front of me. The bumpiness of the afternoon air was getting to me. Playing a mental game with myself, I decided I would crane my neck to see where we were. I promised myself that if we were past the halfway point (which we surely had to be), I would hold it in until we landed. When I looked out the window and saw we were nowhere near half way, my spirits dropped and my stomach rose. I elbowed my friend Elizabeth, sitting beside me, and glared at the plastic bag on her lap containing her camera. "I need that bag," I mumbled, trying to move my mouth as little as possible. With Olympian speed she spilled out the contents and stuffed the plastic in my face, just in time to catch the main event. Excellent timing, but the bag had a hole in it.

I seem to be plagued with such incidents. I think they contribute to my success as a guide. My guests are seldom short of something to laugh about as long as I'm around.

My attention came back to the view as an important and unique landmark emerged out of the broad U-shaped valley below: the Tufa Mounds, three 27-metre domes of soft calcium, ornately sculpted and glistening in the light. The shimmering hotspring emerging from the vent of the active mound was reflecting a crimson sunset. Camera shutters continued to click and whir and I passed the word up the line that we would visit the mounds tomorrow.

The bench lands above the river were dotted with small thermalkarst lakes, caused by the ground warming and the underlying permafrost melting. When this happens, the soil and trees collapse and water collects in the resulting depressions. In the evening light the water was crystal clear and we could see moose tracks on the lake bottoms.

Up ahead the sun's reflection beamed beacon-like off the glassy surface of Rabbitkettle Lake. Just a little further upstream was the riverside gravel bar upon which we would land, below the sharp-spired granite Ragged Range. We rapidly lost altitude and swung over the gravel bar. I could see the group members who had flown in before us. The cerebral orchestra was now pounding strains of Wagner as our quick, helicopter-like descent was broken by the soft balloon tires connecting with the gravel. The reverse thrust of the propellers, (a feature that sets the Twin Otter apart from any other bush plane), brought us to a surprisingly quick yet smooth halt. Not until the co-pilot opened the rear cabin door was the trance broken. We came alive to the hint of the sights, sounds, and smells that waited on the river shore. We quickly unloaded.

Even while our legs were still wobbly from the excitement of the flight, the plane was taxiing away. It lifted off in less distance than seemed possible. To please his audience, our pilot Ted Grant, the owner of Simpson Air, waggled the wings. Circling us, he flew over at tree-top height,

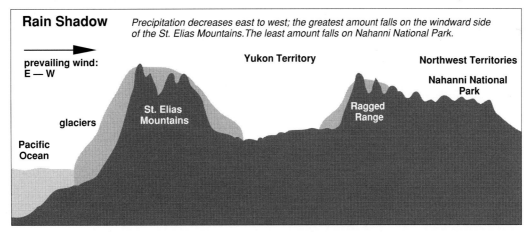

Rain Shadow — *Precipitation decreases east to west; the greatest amount falls on the windward side of the St. Elias Mountains. The least amount falls on Nahanni National Park.*

prevailing wind: E — W

Yukon Territory

Northwest Territories

Nahanni National Park

glaciers

St. Elias Mountains

Ragged Range

Pacific Ocean

TALL MOUNTAINS TO THE WEST CAUSED THE ARID CLIMATE THAT PREVENTED TOTAL GLACIATION OF THE NAHANNI DURING THE LAST ICE AGE.

then sent more than a million dollars' worth of fine-tuned machinery into an impressive climb and away through the peaks. Only the fading drone of the twin turboprops remained as evidence of his having been there at all. The only cargo going back was some postcards Ted promised to mail for one of our party. I learned from him later of the message he had noticed on one of the cards:

> *Flying upriver now through spectacular country. We had to wrestle*
> *the pilot from the local bar and sober him up prior to the flight.*
> *Hope to make it home!…*

In truth Ted and his pilots are relegated to teetotaling through the demanding flying season, but that doesn't scrub away the frontier image attributed to those living on the fringes of Nahanni country.

Some of us a little dazed, we stood there, slowly awakening to the realization that we had lost sight of our only contact with civilization. We were here, relying on the other members of our small group, and that was not going to change for a good while.

On our gravel bar, we were poised just outside the upstream end of Nahanni National Park, yet only half way to the headwaters of the river. Above us lay the wild, technically demanding, and less-travelled waters of the Rock Gardens, reserved for expert whitewater paddlers. They flow from the Moose Ponds, Nahanni's headwaters, where we begin one or two trips each season. The rapids below us within the park provide more than enough excitement for most canoeists.

While the gang was finding their "earth legs" and their packs, my cohort Herb Betsaka and I hustled to finish supper preparations and lend a hand where necessary as folks set up their tents.

In ones and twos, everyone drifted over to the cooking fire and the aroma of shish kebabs. Some of the group pitched in to create a Caesar salad while the others were enjoying freshly brewed coffee. During supper, we talked about what was coming up.

I doled out my standard handy advice:

#1—We were in bear country and caution was in order. Camp was to be kept clean, tents away from the cooking area and food. No food or perfumed material in the tents, including most of the contents of a typical shaving kit. These items could be stored in a box kept with the food supplies. Statistics show that bears are intimidated by groups of four or more. This pointed toward the wisdom of travelling as a group and keeping up the chatter when in the bush so as not to surprise a wandering bruin.

#2—Sanitary concerns. The Nahanni has remained virtually and remarkably free of contamination. This is mainly because of the awareness of the people who travel her valleys. Unfortunately, the insidious and dreaded plague of intestinal parasites that has hit most of North America's wilderness is a potential threat even here. To preserve this pristine country, we always make small pit toilets, burn any toilet paper, and bury any remaining toilet waste well away from the water, in the shielding protection of trees.

It was nearly midnight when someone looked at his watch in the soft daylight. The midnight sun is a pleasant convenience, eliminating the need for flashlights and lanterns until late in August. Gradually the group turned in and the circle around the fire diminished. On my way to my tent, I saw Herb on the shore, silhouetted against the river, surveying the view, listening, taking it all in.

Herb is the youngest of eleven children. He was raised in the tiny village of Nahanni Butte on the banks of the Nahanni in view of its confluence with the mighty Liard. He seems to love sharing his river. He is a Dene Native, who has trapped, hunted, and travelled through Nahanni country. For two years he worked as a trainee with the National Park, but disenchanted with the amount of time spent on government administrivia, Herb was lured to guiding.

Herb's life has been dictated by the seasons. If you ask him when moose-hunting season begins, his answer will involve when the aspen leaves drop instead of calendar dates. Herb has trapped to support his family and knows the frustration of a falling fur market. Hunting helps to fill the family larder. He speaks intensely of the respect his father taught him for the animals he pursues.

He displays this intimacy daily as he interprets the stories told by tracks left on the beach. Details such as species, sex, size, travelling speed, and who was chasing whom can all be gleaned from Herb's keen observations. Spotting Herb crouched over on the shore during a lunch stop becomes a cue to gather 'round and find out what drama has been played out this time.

Standing by the river he looked like he was at home, like he belonged.

At 7:00 a.m. the July sun had already been up for hours. A few of the gang were up and the smell of coffee wafted through camp. The morning light highlighted new aspects of the Ragged Range. We breakfasted on fresh fruit and muffins. We had to enjoy the fresh produce while it lasted.

With guidance provided as required, the group loaded the 5.5-metre ABS plastic canoes, perfectly suited for river travel, and tied the gear securely. A system of rope loops spaced at intervals along the gunnels allowed for easy lacing of the quarter-inch nylon cargo rope. The loading strategy is critical to safety. We made sure that in the event of an upset the load would remain intact. Loose items become a hazard that may wrap around legs, and even if they don't, you're in trouble if you lose your gear in the water. For items needed during the paddle, a waterproofed day pack was positioned within reach. A 20-metre floating synthetic line stuffed into a nylon "throw bag" was placed under a stretchy rubber cord on the stern deck of each canoe. Over the years these rigs have been invaluable for quickly towing upset canoes into shore. When all was in order we pushed off into the river.

Most of our group were new to canoeing on rivers. Herb and I paddled separate canoes, each with a partner. We watched the procession closely, offering instruction to anyone who seemed to require it. There were some green canoeists in the group whom we had paired with more-experienced partners. Everyone looked like they could benefit from the next three days of flat meandering river—a chance to resurrect forgotten skills or learn the latest techniques. This is part of the beauty of the National Park portion of the river: with good leadership, canoeists of almost any background can enjoy its waters.

Soon we pulled in below a gravel shoal along the willow-lined right bank. A small clearing and a yellow-on-brown sign were all that marked the trail into Rabbitkettle Lake. We secured the boats and grabbed lunch and day-hiking gear before hitting the trail. The 0.7-kilometre walk took us over a height of land and through a dry aspen forest. Charred logs showed the area had seen a fire within the last thirty years. After a pleasant tramp, we arrived on the shore of Rabbitkettle Lake near the seasonal park warden's small cabin.

HERB BETSAKA INTERPRETS WOLF
TRACKS ON THE BEACH.

— WOLFGANG WEBER

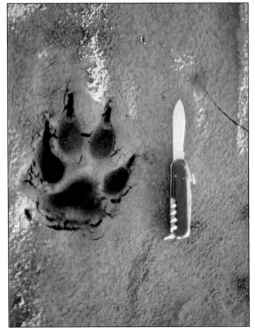

WOLF TRACKS.

— WOLFGANG WEBER

BLACK BEAR TRACKS.

— WOLFGANG WEBER

Moose antler and a cluster of butterflies.

— *Henry Madsen*

Grizzly bear roaming the shore of the Upper Nahanni. The Nahanni Valley is home to moose, dall sheep, mountain caribou, wolf, coyote, mule deer, wolverine, grizzly and black bear, to name a few.

Chapter Three

SECRETS OF THE MILLENNIA

We had been allowed to live for a little time in a world apart—
a lonely world of surpassing beauty, that had given us all things from the
sombre magnificence of the canyons to the gay sunshine of those
wind-swept uplands; from the quiet of the dry side canyons to the uproar
of the broken waters—a land where men pass, and the silence falls
back into place behind them.
— From *The Dangerous River*

The Rabbitkettle warden station is a small prefabricated cedar cabin, set off by a flagpole flying the Canadian maple leaf. With the jagged teeth of the Ragged Range in the distance and softer hills in the foreground it's easy to imagine whiling away all of the summers of your life here without want. You can see this reflected in the attitudes of the wardens, whose 14-day stints at the lake are never long enough. While at the lake they perform a valuable function, guiding passing travellers to the rare and protected Tufa Mounds.

On the three-kilometre hike to the Tufa Mounds we passed a beautiful blue-green pond appropriately named Emerald Lake. This is a pseudokarst feature, formed by the piping sinkhole process, in which water passes through channels in the ground mechanically eroding caverns which collapse leaving lakes. The Tufa Mounds, in contrast, are true karst features because they are formed through a chemical process by water-soluble minerals.

The mounds are a powerful sight, each being half the size of a football field.

Rising near the course of the Rabbitkettle River, the hills of soft tufa were created by the spring water issuing from the geothermal vent in each mound. The secret of their creation lies in the fact that the warm water contains no sulphur. Dissolved calcium carbonate is therefore able to precipitate as a solid, something impossible at sulphur hotsprings elsewhere in the valley.

The process is evident at the northern mound nearest the river, which is still active. A mound begins modestly as calcium-laden water gathers in a pool. At the edge of the puddle a delicate rim of calcium is formed, allowing the water to deepen. These "rimstone dams" evolve into larger "gowers" bordering large, deep pools. Given approximately 10 thousand years, a tufa mound becomes a collection of intricate, terraced, and delicate shapes. Shimmering rivulets of water trickle down its slopes. The earth's warmth keeps the spring at an average temperature of 21 degrees Celsius.

It is thought that the water follows a clockwise course as it flows down around the dome from the vent. As it passes, it lays down new calcium structures, increasing the size of the mound, and painting it in earth tones of ochre, tawny, whites, and greys.

AN AERIAL VIEW OF THE
LARGEST OF THE TUFA
MOUNDS. THE WATER MARKS
INDICATE THE ACTIVE
GROWING PORTION.

— NAHANNI NATIONAL
PARK PHOTO

INSETS:
— TERRY AND LISA PALECHUK

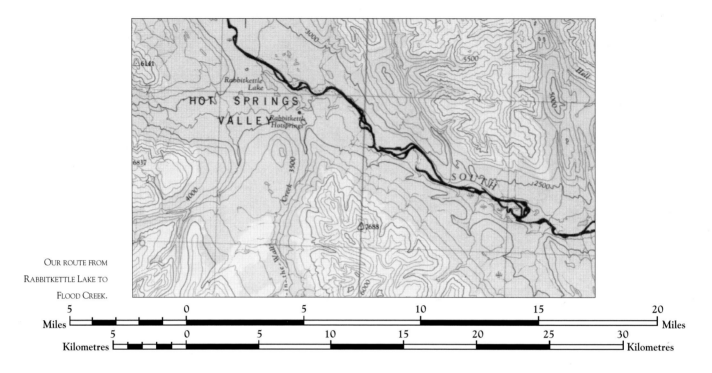

Our route from
Rabbitkettle Lake to
Flood Creek.

These treasures are the largest of their kind in Canada. The National Park administration has designated them a Zone 1 area, which is the most sensitive rating given a natural feature. This means that visitors are allowed access only when escorted by a park warden. The wardens' wealth of knowledge erases any sense of imposition on our wilderness experience, and the hike to the mounds becomes a discovery time for everyone.

After crossing the Rabbitkettle River on a cabled boat, we followed a circuitous route to the mounds, admiring every aspect of the natural sculptures. The north face of the amalgamated mounds has frost-fractured, and the resulting fragments have been naturally sorted where they lie into a series of frost polygons. Frost polygons are a curiosity of the North: repeated freezing and thawing sorts the debris, coaxing the coarse fragments to the perimeter and fine pieces to the centre.

As we circled the Tufa Mounds, I could not help but think of a huge wizard's cauldron that had boiled over and frozen in time. When I gingerly climbed barefoot to the top, the impression was strengthened by the sobering presence of tiny skeletons, leftovers from ravens and raptors who enjoy a dining room with a view.

The large vent lured me to its edge to gaze into the darkness. I struggled between the curious urge to explore its depths and the childlike fear that the resident gargoyle of the depths might rush forth to claim his toll for passage through this spirit-filled land.

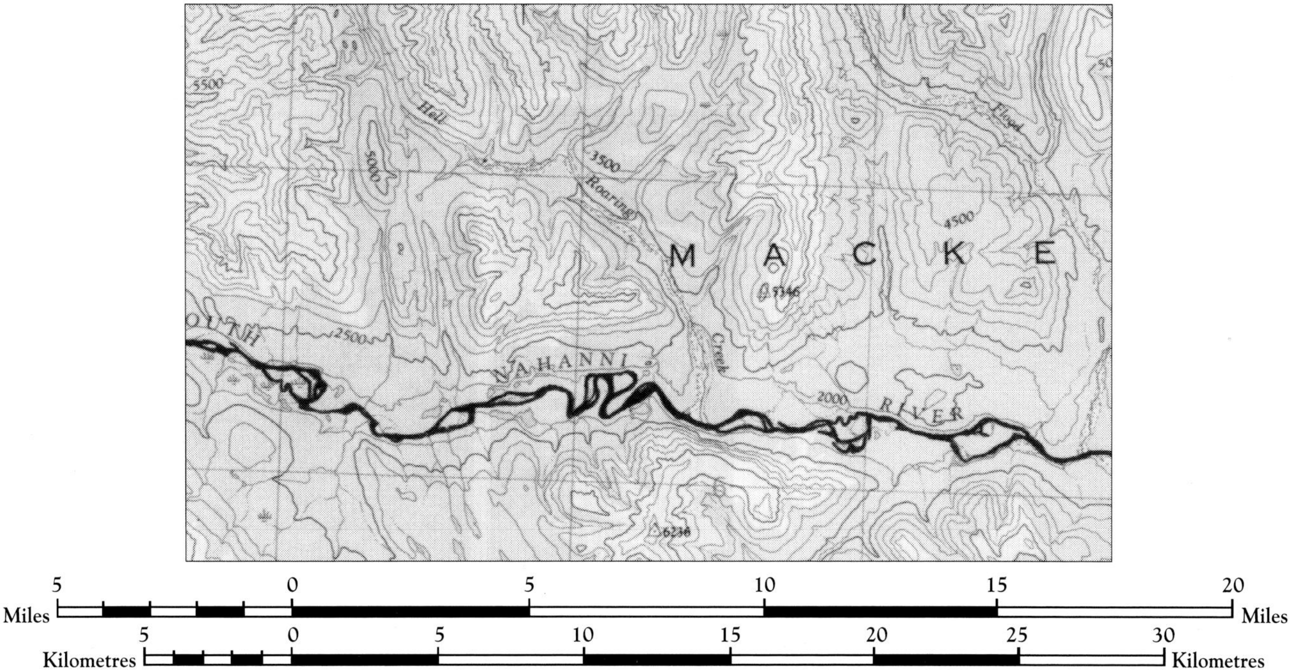
Hell
Roaring
Creek
M A C K E
NAHANNI
RIVER
5 0 5 10 15 20
Miles
5 0 5 10 15 20 25 30
Kilometres

We lingered as long as we could, admiring the 360-degree panorama. The tiny rimstone features felt good under our bare feet. Regulations prohibit shoes of any sort, since they would wear down the delicate surface, obliterating centuries of deposition.

Herb taught us the Slavey name Gogeliąh for the hotsprings. When travelling through the area, his ancestors made pilgrimages to the mounds. They considered it a bad omen if the vent was not brim-full with water.

Looking upriver from where we stood, we could see the jagged peaks of the Ragged Range and the Hole in the Wall Lake area. To understand the lay of the land one must imagine the scenery between 550 and 200 million years ago, when the region was part of a large, tropical, continental ocean shelf. Under the tremendous pressure of the sea, sands became sandstones and muds became shales. Cemented by precipitated carbonate, skeletons of marine animals became limestone. Some limestone hardened into dolomites. The seas dried up, revealing a flat plain stretching to the horizon.

Then about 200 million years ago, the mountain-building process began. Igneous batholiths—huge conglomerations of molten rock within the earth—pushed upwards to become hard granite intrusions in the earth's crust. These lifted up and deformed the sedimentary rock above. At the same time, the continental shelf collided with the oceanic plate to the west and overrode it, creating the cordillera chain of mountain ranges that stretches from Mexico to the

THIS ALUMINUM BOAT
ATTACHED TO A CABLE, FERRIES
ACROSS THE RABBITKETTLE
RIVER TO THE TUFFA MOUNDS.

— HENRY MADSEN

Arctic. The razor-sharp peaks evident today were revealed by gradual erosion of the softer, over-lying rock.

The upheaval of the batholiths created the softer, sedimentary mountain ranges over which we had flown. Like ripples in a pond, these mountains extend east, ending abruptly at the plains of the Liard River.

Between eight and two million years ago continental drift carried this area northward into a colder climate. Ice, wind, and water shaped the land.

From where we stood on the mounds, we could see evidence of the geological saga that followed. The young Nahanni River fashioned for itself a steep-sided, narrow, V-shaped valley, but now, looking towards the Nahanni and the mountains on the far shore, the valley has an obvious "U" shape, indicating glacial carving. Two major ice bodies bracketed this area in the last ice period: the "Cordilleran," which emanated from the western mountains, and the "Laurentide" from the plains of the east. But the middle portion of Nahanni National Park was spared from both, and the portion of the valley where we were standing was likely visited only by some of the earlier Cordilleran advances beginning about two million years ago.

While most of Canada experienced four ice advances, this region lacked the necessary precipitation and was spared the last one, the Wisconsin, occurring between eighty thousand and eight thousand years ago. During this time, though, the valley flooded because the Laurentide ice formed a barrier to the east at the mouth of the Nahanni. The river backed up to form Glacial Lake Nahanni twice during the Wisconsin, and once to form the shallower Glacial Lake

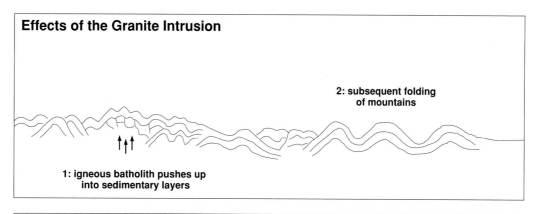

Effects of the Granite Intrusion

2: subsequent folding
of mountains

1: igneous batholith pushes up
into sedimentary layers

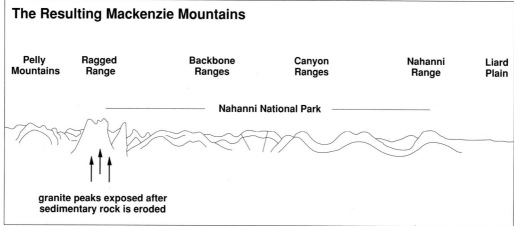

The Resulting Mackenzie Mountains

| Pelly Mountains | Ragged Range | Backbone Ranges | Canyon Ranges | Nahanni Range | Liard Plain |

Nahanni National Park

granite peaks exposed after
sedimentary rock is eroded

THE UPTHRUST OF THE IGNEOUS BATHOLITH AND SUBSEQUENT FOLDING FORMED THE MOUNTAINS IN THE NAHANNI REGION.

Tetcella. Each of these massive lakes likely lasted ten thousand years.

We took a comfortable dip in the hotspring-warmed lake when we returned to the cabin. After a brief registration procedure with the park warden, we made our way back to the boats and embarked on the river once again.

The surprisingly swift current whisked us along. Someone pointed towards a raven perched on a rock, whose behaviour puzzled us all. With rhythmic precision he was slamming his head downwards, seemingly trying to split the boulder with his beak. As we floated closer the mystery was solved. The rock was the carcass of a dead mountain caribou, and the raven was trying to tear through the hide and get at the meal awaiting below. "Bon appetit" was our farewell as we drifted by. The raven is a coy bird who deserves courtesy in all discourse lest you return to camp some day after a hike and find he has ravaged your camp more thoroughly than any bear could hope to do.

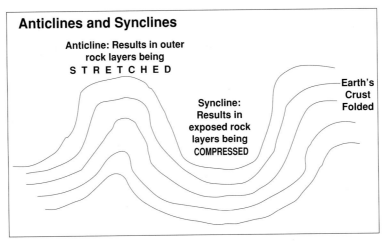

Anticlines and Synclines

Anticline: Results in outer rock layers being **S T R E T C H E D**

Syncline: Results in exposed rock layers being COMPRESSED

Earth's Crust Folded

THE DIFFERENCE BETWEEN AN ANTICLINE AND A SYNCLINE AND THE RESULTING STRETCHING OR COMPRESSING OF OUTER ROCK LAYERS.

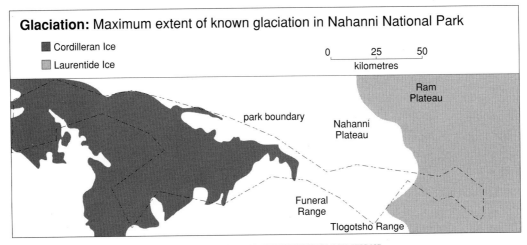

Glaciation: Maximum extent of known glaciation in Nahanni National Park

■ Cordilleran Ice
▨ Laurentide Ice

0   25   50
kilometres

Ram Plateau

park boundary

Nahanni Plateau

Funeral Range

Tlogotsho Range

THE UNGLACIATED REGION BETWEEN THE WESTERN CORDILLERAN ICE AND THE EASTERN LAURENTIDE ICE.

Paddling leisurely for five kilometres brought us to a broad gravel bar with plenty of drift wood, which I chose to believe was deposited thoughtfully by the spring flood in consideration of our need for a cooking fire.

We all felt like we'd had a full day, particularly after the globe-trotting that had brought us together. Herb and I hustled the kitchen affairs into shape while the others picked flat, sandy spots for their tents.

I like to tell our staff that guiding is 95 per cent cooking, 5 per cent terror. Herb and I started the supper.

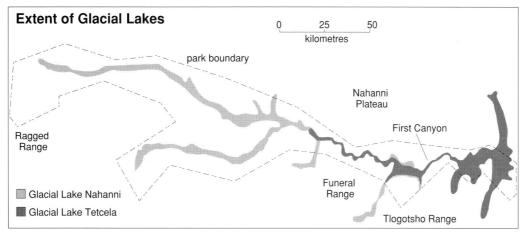

Extent of Glacial Lakes

0   25   50
kilometres

park boundary

Ragged
Range

Nahanni
Plateau

First Canyon

Funeral
Range

Tlogotsho Range

☐ Glacial Lake Nahanni
■ Glacial Lake Tetcela

THE EXTENT OF THE GLACIAL LAKES CREATED AT DIFFERENT PERIODS WHEN THE DOWNSTREAM END OF THE RIVER WAS BLOCKED BY LAURENTIDE ICE.

We usually draw our water straight from the river. The main channel is coloured a deep green by silty rock flour from the glaciers. Despite its colour, the water tastes fresh and clean. It's some comfort that this type of silt is used in commercial coffee whitener. In recent years we have taken to purifying all the water we drink; no one wants to be the first to learn that a micro-organism has been introduced. The resulting intestinal liquefaction is no joke. For some it may only mean a month of severe discomfort and weakness. In the most extreme cases it can result in death. We use chemical purification, but commercial filters can be purchased for the same purpose, or you can boil your drinking water for five minutes.

We got a fire started in the portable fire box. Although scars from fires built on the sand below the high water mark are washed away in the spring, it isn't fair to leave fire scars for groups coming through later in the summer. The Outfitters Association has donated a number of these boxes to the park so that even private travellers are issued them before going into the wilderness.

Talk around the campfire ranged far and wide, as it always does. Glacier Lake, upstream from our camp, was the scene of an unsettling story that had to be told. In February 1936 two partners, Bill Epler and Joe Mullholland, were flown into the country from Nahanni Butte to trap and prospect. When they failed to return the following summer, George Dalziel, a bush pilot, flew in to look for them. All that he could find were the burned-out remains of their cabin at Glacier Lake; two more to add to the tally of missing souls in the Nahanni country.

It wasn't long before someone asked me if I had known any of the legendary figures of the river. In truth, many of them were gone before I came along. Albert Faille, Raymond Patterson, Charles Yohin, Ted Trindell, Dick Turner, and others, all gone, but I had become friends with one of the legends a decade earlier, and he was one of the most impressive men I have known. I set out to answer the question.

Chapter Four

LIVING LEGENDS

There's a land that where the mountains are nameless,
And the rivers all run God knows where;
There are lives that are erring and aimless,
And deaths that just hang by a hair,
There are hardships that nobody reckons;
There are valleys unpeopled and still;
There's a land – oh, it beckons and beckons,
And I want to go back – and I will.
— From *The Spell of the Yukon* by Robert Service

It was below Second Canyon in Deadmen Valley, on my first Nahanni adventure, that I met Father Pierre Mary OMI—the only individual I've ever met who had his picture in the National Geographic. This humble man was the stuff of legends. A member of the French Underground during the Second World War, he emerged from the experience with a desire to serve humanity. Since 1955 at the age of 28, he had lived in the North as an Oblate. For many years he was completely dependent on river boats and dog-teams to visit his parishioners. He was fluent in Slavey. The facial scars incurred years ago tormented him in the winter's cold but he was undaunted in serving his people.

We first met during an RCMP patrol into the Nahanni area. So esteemed was his knowledge of the river that the police chose him to pilot their craft through the canyons. As chance would have it, I was camped with friends in Deadmen Valley, and after introductions my cohorts and I listened spellbound to Father Mary's tales of his early days in the North.

He would make his round of visits by dog-team in the winter, taking five days to cover the distance one way. These huskies were not the pet-shop variety; they strode the fine line between working dog and wild animal. Intricate psychology was required to keep them on your side.

He told of the predicament he sometimes faced while camped on the trail if one of the dogs got loose from his chain during the night. The loose dog would wind the rest of the dogs into a howling frenzy, but chasing after a loose husky in the dark of a forty-below night would be folly. Such is their sense of play that they would lead you on for miles, always just a few paces ahead. If, through some stroke of luck, you managed to grab him, you might not survive your success. There was a far simpler and more amusing solution.

Crawling reluctantly out of his sleeping bag, he would take each of the other dogs, one by one, and put them in their spots in the harness on the sled. When the last captive dog was hitched up, the ranging loner would be at Father Mary's heels, whimpering to be included in his

DeHAVILLAND BEAVER FLOAT

PLANE LANDING ON

RABBITKETTLE LAKE.

rightful spot in the harness. These dogs live to pull; it's in their blood. A good dog handler will spend much more time feeding and tending to his dogs each evening—rewarding this dedication—than he will taking care of himself. If not caught quickly, a lone dog would follow the trail back to the village. Awaiting it would be certain death. Since they were so closely related to wolves, roaming sled dogs were hunting animals—real threats to children and even chained dogs. When they approached the village they would be shot.

One night while tending to his dogs at his cabin in the village Father Mary noticed that one of them had crapped in a frying pan being used as a dog bowl, and the mess had frozen hard. He couldn't even chisel it from the pan. He took the pan into the cabin to thaw and placed it on the counter, then promptly went back to work. Later in the evening a friend came by to visit. During the visit he must have caught sight of the frying pan. With a concerned look and sincere tone the friend said, "Father, do you have enough food?"

Father Mary happened to be on the river during the most impressive flood in recent history. While returning from the Flat River country during an unusually rainy spell, the water rose more than 20 vertical feet overnight. This flash flood created large standing waves at the normally calm Pulpit Rock, flooded the sprawling Prairie Creek alluvial fan in Deadmen Valley, and topped the opposite bank. Somehow Father Mary managed to manœuvre his flat-bottomed scow back to Nahanni Butte, and, feeling lucky to be alive, he retired to his cabin to rest from the ordeal. After he awoke, realizing what a near miss he had survived, he went down to his boat to retrieve his gear. As he stepped into the craft it began to disintegrate under his weight. Barely managing to hop back to shore before it totally broke up, he collapsed on his knees, counting his blessings.

I became good friends with Father Mary. One could not help but respect the man.

The same trip on which I met Father Mary—my first trip on the Nahanni—was filled with adventure. Within the space of three weeks I was involved in a cops-and-robbers pursuit, a near grizzly encounter, and savage head-hunters.

I was on this particular trip at the invitation of Rick Driediger, a friend from northern Saskatchewan. In preparation for the adventure I had read The Dangerous River by R.M. Patterson. He wrote, "Men vanish in that country. There were some prospectors murdered in there not so long ago and down the river they say it is a damned good country to keep clear of...." Not being one to swallow this sort of story hook, line, and sinker, I wrote off the ominous title as a ploy to sell books. I was soon proved wrong.

We began at Rabbitkettle Lake. I was spellbound by the scenery and didn't pay much heed to Patterson's words—that is until we got to Virginia Falls. We laid over a few days to absorb the magnificence of the falls, which are more than twice the height of Niagara, and to take in some of the side attractions.

Before long we were joined by the "prospectors," as we came to refer to them: four husky young fellows from a big city in the United States. They claimed to be following in the footsteps of their "Grampy." He had left the Nahanni with $32 thousand worth of gold back in '52, they said.

FATHER MARY OMI AND HIS
SLED DOG "GRIZZLY".

— WENDELL E. WHITE COLLECTION

RICHARDSONS GROUND SQUIRREL WITH A COMMANDING VIEW FROM SUNBLOOD MOUNTAIN.
— TERRY PALECHUK

When we first met the prospectors, they were anxious to fill us in on their plans. It seemed they had never paddled a canoe before. This was OK, because they planned to prospect at the falls for four months, until the river level subsided. "At that time of year a guy can scoop up the nuggets lyin' in front of the rocks!" A nice plan, but illegal in Nahanni National Park.

We soon began to have doubts about the outlook for their trip when rumblings reached us from their nearby camp. A black eye and cut forehead the next morning looked a lot like they had survived an axe fight cum fist fight.

By the time we left the falls we decided that if they didn't finish each other off, the river surely would. We didn't expect to lay eyes on them again.

Unbeknown to us, within a few days the prospectors had their fill of the Canadian North and immediately began to bungle their way down Fourth Canyon. Two of them got dumped while negotiating the tricky canyon, and their companions just laughed as they cruised by and left them to rescue themselves.

The prospectors camped that night at the Big Bend of the Nahanni. A beautiful location with steep canyon walls, it was also the choice of six members of the Canadian Armed Forces out on adventure training. These fellows were strapping examples of all that is good and patriotic—in short,the antithesis of the prospectors. The two parties kept a respectable distance and each quietly tolerated the other's presence. All was well until around 2:00 a.m. when one of the prospectors, drunk, decided to see how well rifle shots would echo in the canyons of the Big Bend.

The soldiers in their own words, "weren't sticking around with lunatics like that." They moved their camp to a new position, which they camouflaged. They also posted a guard for the night. The prospectors immediately realized they had been bad boys. The four later reported they had never seen anyone break camp as quickly as the soldiers had. It took only seconds.

As soon as they raised their groggy heads the next morning, the prospectors made great haste paddling downriver, worrying that the soldiers would radio the wardens about the night before. Their prediction was correct, as we learned the next morning when the soldiers and wardens showed up simultaneously at our camp in Deadmen Valley.

As our party left for Kraus Hotsprings we were certain that the prospectors were no match for the wardens' jet boat.

A sulphurous odour greeted us at the springs. After pitching camp above the beach, the two other fellows in our group went back into the lush bush in search of other springs. That left the three girls and me to soak in the pools on the beach.

No sooner had we reclined in the luxurious pools than we spotted two familiar canoes rounding the distant bend. You can imagine our feelings when we recognized our prospector friends. Naturally they were anxious to bend our ears about how they had "eluded the law" all day long. They were bragging before they got out of the canoes. Their strategy, they explained, had been to "pull off the river and hightail it for the bush" whenever they heard the approaching jet boat.

The four soon retired to the clearing above the river bank to rest before unloading their boats. They were nervous and exhausted from their flight from "the law," and we didn't help any by telling them the legend of the head-hunting savages of Deadmen Valley (which I think they took for gospel).

In the meantime our boys had made a find in the depths of the hottest of the pools. Black, gooey mud that stuck nicely to your skin. The fellows thought it would be a terrific joke to smear themselves with mud, arm themselves with spears and surprise us on the beach. They had no idea that the prospectors had arrived at our camp.

The meeting of the prospectors and our "savages" had to be the most bizarre scene on the

THE GHASTLY APPARITIONS OF THE HOTSPRING.

Nahanni since the McLeod brothers lost their heads in '06.

Our savages mistook the prospectors' sincere looks of fear for jest and so proceeded to ham it up by giving chase. The prospectors fled for their lives yelling, "Get the gun! Get the gun!"

From the pools on the beach we heard the commotion. We were certain that a grizzly was after the prospectors and feared that it may have already mauled our companions back in the bush.

Four blurred figures flashed by towards the prospectors' canoes, still yelling "Get the gun! Get the gun!" Tearing the spray decks off their boats they frantically searched for their precious rifle.

A split second later we turned to see our spear-wielding savages, darker than our cooking pots. At our uproarious laughter the four prospectors became confused and stopped searching for their gun. Then they began to laugh, nervously at first, while our laughter diminished. It began to dawn on us that our boys had probably come within seconds of becoming dead meat! The renegades would have had no qualms about ridding the Canadian North of a couple of dangerous savages.

Shortly, however, the hilarity of the situation took over again. As the prospectors headed back to their campsite, one was still holding his chest from the excitement.

Then, like the cavalry coming over the hill in the movies, the wardens and their jet boat appeared from around the bend. The jig was up for our friends. After a confrontation and some discussion the wardens politely relieved them of their rifle.

We didn't see the prospectors leave the next morning, but I imagine it was with great haste. Apparently they showed up in Nahanni Butte at 11:00 p.m. that night demanding their rifle. They had made good time for beginners.

I'm sure that the next scene took place in a big American barroom. Our four prospectors were most likely standing on a table, crowds gathered quietly around, all listening in awe to tales of Nahanni savages, shooting at the Canadian Army, and eluding the law in the rugged Canadian North.

It's still a dangerous river!

Chapter Five

GOING WITH THE FLOW

*Those of us who had the good fortune to be on the South Nahanni in those
last days of the old North may, in times of hunger or hardship, have cursed
the day we ever heard the name of that fabled river. Yet a treasure was ours
in the end: memories of a carefree time and an utter and absolute freedom
which the years cannot dim nor the present age provide.*
— From *The Dangerous River*

The following morning, our group left our camp below the Tufa Mounds. We were back on the river. Generally three hours pass between the time we rise and when we first dip our paddles in the current. Early risers may put on the coffee, wet a fishing line, or capture the early morning light on film. Breakfast is usually ready around 8:00 a.m. Then cleaning and packing up begins and doesn't end until the campsite looks the way we found it.

Shortly after leaving camp we passed a bare, smooth, canoe-length log, breaking the surface in midstream. Undulating with the relentless current at a shallow downstream angle, the stout pole uttered a sea monster's dull roar as it repeatedly dipped below the surface and rose again. I thought back to an evening camp slightly upstream, almost a decade earlier. We had been alarmed by a noise, thinking it was some marauding animal. Since then, seasons of winter ice more than a metre thick, spring break-ups, and the following floods had not served to dislodge this old tree from the river bottom. We skittered past admiring the forceful dance as the log tried to teach us about the unseen, relentless power of the current. Lessons like this one are abundant and often deceptively simple. Wilderness schooling is never complete.

The river below Rabbitkettle Lake increases its meandering as it decreases in velocity above the cataract of Virginia Falls. The two days I usually take to cover the 118 kilometres are generally the longest stretches of paddling on this piece of the river, but the rugged sedimentary mountain ranges to left and right and the anticipation of the faster water in the canyons below keep the paddlers inspired.

The broad valley here is home to an assortment of wildlife. Moose, wolves, black bears, and grizzly bears are all common. Raptors such as the bald eagle may be seen, perched sentry-like above a favourite fishing hole, or in a huge nest of sticks in the top of an ancient cottonwood, overlooking the river. On one occasion we spotted a small "V" shape on the surface of the water, pointing upstream as you would expect behind a submerged branch. Curiously, it was moving laterally across the river. As we neared it, the "branch" became a squirrel dog-paddling across the river. We watched with incredulous fascination until she finally reached the other side and scrambled up the bank and into a spindly black spruce.

A SEPTEMBER EVENING IN
FIRST CANYON.

— WOLFGANG WEBER

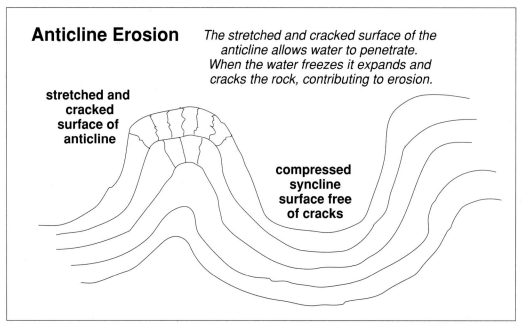

Anticline Erosion

The stretched and cracked surface of the anticline allows water to penetrate. When the water freezes it expands and cracks the rock, contributing to erosion.

stretched and cracked surface of anticline

compressed syncline surface free of cracks

ANTICLINES ARE MORE PRONE TO FROST CRACKING AND RELATED EROSION THAN SYNCLINES BECAUSE OF THE CRACKS IN THE STRETCHED SURFACE.

We ate lunch while floating, enjoying the warm sun and allowing the river to carry us closer to our destination while we relaxed. With the canoes rafted together, lunch was passed around along with jokes and comments about the scenery we were passing. A common theme—the similarity between the tree line and my hair line—supplied much of the humour. Once everyone's appetite was satisfied, Herb took over steering the raft of canoes. We got comfortable, using packs as back rests. Soon the atmosphere was quiet except for an occasional snore, later blamed on me. After 20 minutes or so of this digestive activity, bodies resurrected. Soon we were six separate canoes, once again propelling ourselves towards the falls.

The slower meandering nature of the river here is deceptive. As we rounded a bend in the river, I was reminded of a small log cabin that had been built on the outside bank earlier in the century by an unknown prospector. Originally the cabin was 15 metres back in the bush, a short walk from the shore. By the early '80s the river had eroded the bank to the point where the cabin was teetering over the stream. Finally, the cabin disappeared into the green current, demonstrating the relentless power of the river. This same power created the many "sweepers" that line the river's shore. These are trees, usually on outside bends, that have been undermined by the current until they hang precariously over the water, sometimes partly submerged. These, combined with log jams composed chiefly of former sweepers, are the greatest hazard to a canoeist. We take great

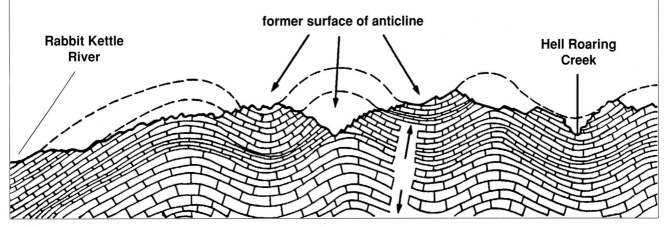

Inverted Topography

Water penetrates easily into the surface of an anticline. When the water freezes, it expands and cracks the rock. This hastens erosion and causes the inverted topography shown here.

former surface of anticline

Rabbit Kettle River

Hell Roaring Creek

<small>ANTICLINE EROSION LEADS TO EARLIER EROSION OF THE TALLER STRUCTURES.</small>

care to give these obstacles a wide berth, and we enforce a strict policy of wearing lifejackets at all times. Mountain rivers demand this kind of respect. There is no such thing as a stretch of river free of hazard, and the paddler does well to accept this maxim without question.

We took a leg-stretching break at Hell Roaring Creek. Looking up the creek valley, we saw the unusual aftermath of the geological folding process. The entire Hell Roaring Creek valley had been the heart of a vast anticline. Because the outer layers of the anticline were stretched further than the inner layers, they were cracked. Over the ages, the freezing and thawing of moisture in the cracks resulted in more fracturing. As time passed, the fractured rock eroded away the heart of the anticline, leaving the lower but better-preserved synclines on either side. Now the revealed edges of these ancient synclines form the higher peaks along the valley.

Late that day we camped downriver of Flood Creek on another broad sand bar with a panoramic view of the surrounding peaks. Camp routine had already become ritualistic. In the "kitchen," Herb set up the box-like folding ovens over the gas stove and prepared to bake two cakes for dessert. In the morning the same ovens would yield golden, sticky, cinnamon buns. We talked of Virginia Falls, which was within one day's paddle. The gentle evening breeze was decidedly downstream, which probably indicated a change in the weather.

Although everyone was a little tired, spirits remained good. I was confident that the Nahanni was doing its job of keeping group morale high and that neither Herb nor I would be required to perform any arbitration duties within the group. We seldom are. I think this is partly

CINNAMON BUNS AND BREAD IN THE FOLDING OVENS.
— HENRY MADSEN

true because of the type of person who tends to gravitate towards such an experience: good-natured, flexible, and in general looking for a good time in a beautiful place.

Our guests are inspiring people. We have a loyal following who come from all walks of life. There are no pretensions in the levelling environment of a wilderness trip. Someone who drives a Rolls Royce will paddle with a Volkswagen owner. Our trip lists often read like Who's Who. Another saving factor is group size. With 10 to 12 participants being usual, there is "social room" within the group. Interaction is diffused enough that a person can slip away unnoticed for some quiet time without starting an inquisition. For a guide, this is a blessing. There are countless horror stories of trips with good friends gone sour. I happened upon one such trip a few years ago. A group of four friends were travelling on their own after planning their dream trip for years.

The group had become fragmented. The fellow who had been the catalyst for the planning and who had shouldered most of the preparation was now being shunned by his comrades. This was obvious to us when we met them in passing at Kraus Hotsprings. Later on in the season we learned the clique's fate from the wardens.

To appreciate what happened you have to understand that the Nahanni has a fast watershed—meaning that water from storms quickly funnels down from the surrounding mountains and increases the river level very dramatically. During rainy weather, travellers have to be alert to this fact and plan accordingly.

During a particularly wet spell they pulled in to camp on Swan Point, a long, sandy, gooseneck in the Liard River below the confluence of the Nahanni. Things had worsened among the members and the shunned fellow was now relegated to his own tent while the other three slept together. While taking a leak during the night, the lone camper saw that the river was rising and would soon be lapping at the tents. His warning to the other tent was greeted by, "Leave us alone and go back to sleep!". Feeling that he had done his duty, he packed up his own gear, secured it in the canoe and sat and watched as the waters surrounded the sound sleepers. The four all survived the trip, but their friendship didn't.

PANCAKES FOR BREAKFAST.

— WOLFGANG WEBER

HIKING THROUGH
YELLOW DRYAS.

— MORTEN ASFELDT

Chapter Six

Naʔaa Dehé Náįlįcho

Still the greatest canoe trip in the world – the Nahanni River.
— Bill Mason, film maker, artist and author of *Path of the Paddle* in
Deadmen Valley Log Book, August 1985

Morning greeted us with a gun-metal-grey sky. Water droplets on every surface were the tell-tale sign of showers during the night and a betting person would have put money on more during the day. I emerged from my tent to find that camp was quiet and the spitting rain was turning to a drizzle.

The gentle drumming of raindrops on a tent is a lulling sound when heard from within the warm cocoon of a sleeping bag. I didn't need telepathy to know that each person was savouring the last moments in their cozy sleeping bags before emerging into the damp air. While I kindled the fire, Herb and a couple of others erected the large tarp.

My old friend and mentor, Mors Kochanski, had taught me the secret of lighting and maintaining a fire with wet wood. Collect twigs from driftwood trees on the beach whenever possible so that you're ready for the rain. You take a fist-sized bundle of dead twigs, thinner than match sticks, preferably spruce or willow, and flex them in the middle to create a doubled bundle with split middles exposed at the bend. Hold the bundle above a match or lighter flame so that the heat travels up into the bundle, rising through the twigs as if through a chimney. Clutch the bundle firmly so that the space between twigs is no more than the diameter of individual pieces.

Fire requires heat, oxygen and fuel. With practice, this method allows you to control all three to enable combustion in the worst of conditions. Hold the bundle after it ignites until the small flames are nurtured into a little blaze. You won't burn your hand if you manage it properly. Carefully place the burning bundle in the fire box. Pile on pencil-thick pieces liberally followed by thumb-diameter and then wrist-thick pieces. No holding back and no messing around with breaking, sawing or cutting pieces. Feed longer pieces into the heart of the blaze after they are burnt in half. Wet wood dries quickly on such a fire.

Lay a couple of large driftwood logs parallel to contain the blaze and feed it for cooking and heating. Position a grate across them and the cooking fire is ready.

With practice the whole process takes less than five minutes. The key is to use dead wood from above the recent high water mark. Except for the initial supply of kindling, unless you're camping in a rain forest, there is no need to protect firewood from the rain or to precariously perch wood around the fire to dry it out. If you want the stuff dry, throw it on the fire and it will dry and burn in short order. If the wood is truly waterlogged it will feel heavy for its size and

VIRGINIA FALLS FROM
THE FOOT OF SUNBLOOD
MOUNTAIN.

— D. SALAYKA

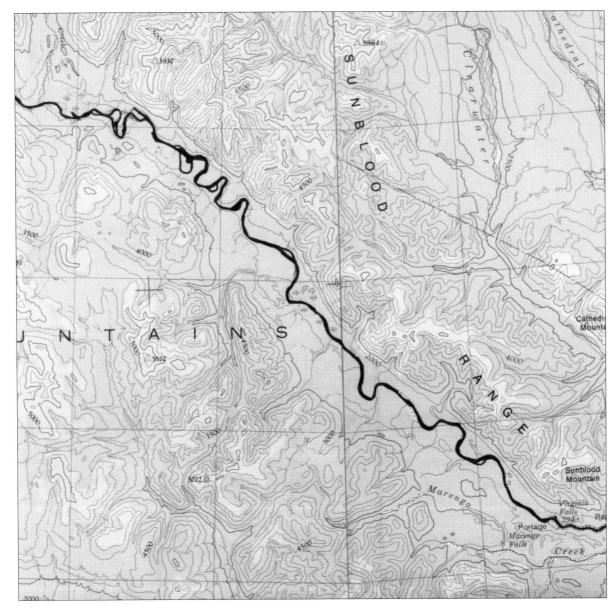

OUR ROUTE FROM
FLOOD CREEK TO
VIRGINIA FALLS.

won't burn no matter what you do.

Wisps of smoke and the smell of coffee drifting across the sand bar gradually lured the last of the roosting campers out of their tents. They congregated by the fire at the edge of the large tarp. More than one of the group commended the tarp architects for their prowess. The shelter was high enough to stand underneath and stout enough to resist the breeze. After a relaxed breakfast of cinnamon buns, we struck camp and loaded the canoes. Clad in rain pants and jackets, we embarked.

I called "Potty break!" as we neared a large alluvial fan. These fan-shaped collections of boulders, gravel, and sand form where tributaries meet the main channel. Some fans are small, but because of the unique history of the Nahanni, others have reached gargantuan proportions. Because the valley has not been scoured by glaciers for more than 100 thousand years, the debris deposited by these tributaries has accumulated to cover many hectares in some cases. The steep valley walls in the area that yield fast flowing, high gradient streams that carry vast amounts of material have also contributed to the size of these alluvial fans.

Back on the river, we could see another secret of the millennia revealed. To the south, a broad pass between two peaks indicated the former path of the river. Glacial ice blocked this route and the subsequent lifting of the land forced the current into its present channel. Irvine Creek, which now occupies the pass, is known as an "underfit" stream because of the imbalance between the size of the valley and the size of the stream.

On the other side of this valley, where Irvine Creek feeds the Flat River, tragedy struck in 1931. Trapper and prospector Phil Powers had built a cabin there. By the spring of 1932, all that remained were the charred remains of the cabin and Power's body. Dick Turner, author of Nahanni, claimed that the remains were identified by gold teeth fillings and a pocket watch. Turner adds that nailed to a tree nearby was a split piece of wood with pencilled words reading, "Phil Powers—his finis."

Above us thick clouds hung low in the valley, passing between and often swallowing the peaks. The river's course was deflected at each alluvial fan, causing it to slow into large meanders with little current. Late in the afternoon, as blue sky patches were becoming dominant, we headed the canoes shoreward into what appeared to be a weed-bound stream. Ten metres' paddling took us into an oxbow lake, formerly a part of the main channel. The ever-increasing looping meander of the river had finally "bitten itself off," allowing the current to flow past instead of around the meander, and leaving behind the oxbow lake. We floated on the stillness of the lake in a spontaneous rest break. The canoes drifted apart on the small body of water. Above the lake, the mountain slope was scarred by a fire in 1981. The tree line on the mountains is quite low here, and the peaks in the immediate area are all bare crags, each with a peculiar shape and character. A few of our group pressed fishing lines into action while others dozed or got out on shore. The afternoon was passing on and we had another 15 kilometres between us and Virginia Falls.

Back in the main channel, our paddles bit the slowing current. Just around the next bend we passed an unoccupied wardens' cabin. We could see sheep trails on the mountainside across the river from the cabin. Trodden for countless generations, these are the trails of Ovis dalli: Dall sheep. Nearly white in colour, the Rams' horns curl outward from the skull, distinguishing them from Rocky Mountain bighorn sheep whose horns curl out less. Surveying the trails with binoculars we soon spotted a ewe and a lamb, nonchalantly nosing among the talus for lichen.

As we pressed on we could see ahead a mountain with a distinct band of red ore running diagonally below the peak. Old-time bush pilot George Dalziel had noted this and named the mountain Sunblood. The falls lie at the base of the mountain.

I could not help but notice the close attention the group was giving to the map. Could it be that they didn't trust my memory for the exact location of the falls? Never! ... well, maybe. After all, since the falls have a total drop of 117 metres and the formidable rapids of the Sluice Box lying at the top, it's easy to see why the group would want to be cautious. For my part I could paddle this part of the river blind, only because the roar of the torrent is an immediate give-away well above the actual hazard.

We finally landed at the campsite above the falls in the early evening. Poor drainage makes most of the surrounding land bad for camping, but the designated spot comprises one large hummock. The falls create a bottleneck here for river trippers, so the park managers have had to "harden" the site with designated tent sites and trails. Permafrost lies below the ground's surface, meaning that only the upper layer of soil thaws in the summer. Damaged foliage does not regenerate quickly in this environment. The hardened campsite prevents the spread of damage.

We picked a site and unloaded the canoes. I happily observed that we were the only group there. A few weeks later and this would not be the case. As on every other river of notoriety in North America—indeed the world—you will likely see other travellers on the Nahanni the middle of the summer. The river sees the greatest visitation in the last week of July and first week of August, so those wishing to avoid other groups should plan to avoid this time. Perhaps the future will see mandatory registration and controlled access.

While Herb and I prepared supper, the group hiked the kilometre to the Sluice Box rapids above the falls. Returning in awe, they talked over supper about the sight they had seen. Sleep came quickly with the soothing sound of the falls in the background.

Gentleman explorer Fenlay Hunter named the falls after his daughter Virginia in 1928. The Falls appeared in Nahanni, the award-winning 1961 National Film Board movie. The film depicted 60-year-old trapper and prospector Albert Faillie on an upriver journey from Fort Simpson to a location above the falls. In spite of all the impressive scenery in the movie, by far the most incredible scene was the portage up and around the falls. Albert had brought enough boards and supplies in his outboard-powered river scow to manufacture a second and smaller boat above the cataract with which to explore the upper river. His challenge was to portage these materials, along with a barrel of gas, an outboard motor, and his camping supplies. With his bent back and aged face, Albert struck a commanding image, taking on a task that would be daunting to people many years his junior.

The movie made Albert out to be seized with gold fever. When my friend Jacques Van Pelt

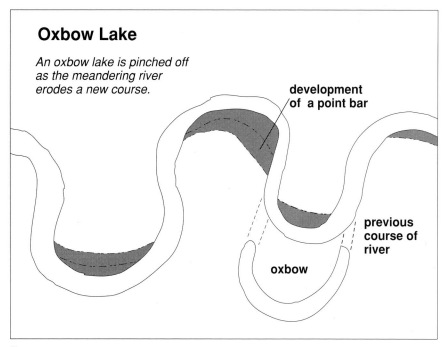

Oxbow Lake

An oxbow lake is pinched off as the meandering river erodes a new course.

development of a point bar

previous course of river

oxbow

THE EVOLUTION OF AN OXBOW LAKE.

screened the movie for Albert after it was first released, Albert was visibly disappointed with the way he had been portrayed. His friends knew him to be a gentle and compassionate person. If any gold possessed him, it was the intangible sort that coloured the hillsides in autumn and painted the winter sunset.

Albert had prospected and trapped in the Nahanni area since 1927, when he began his stay of three consecutive winters in his cabin on the Flat River. Raymond Patterson writes of meeting Albert and learning river skills from him on his first upriver journey. The locals knew Albert as "Red Pant" because of the pants he had made from wool blankets.

Even before his death in Fort Simpson in 1973, Albert had become a Nahanni legend.

Nahʔaa Dehé Náįlicho, or "big water falling," the Dene name for the falls, was the site we chose for a lay-over. After breakfast the next day, those who wished to hike to the top of Sunblood Mountain paddled across the river to where the trail begins. The six-hour hike climbs 960 metres to the 1,500-metre summit. It requires a good level of fitness, lunch, rain gear, and safety equipment. The remainder of the gang chose to spend the day exploring the vast area surrounding the falls and Sluice Box Rapids.

The rapids above the falls are caused by fractures in the limestone river-bed. The results are formidable. A few weeks earlier Paul Jones, a local pilot, had seen a cow and calf moose

THE SLUICE BOX RAPIDS ON
THE BRINK OF VIRGINIA FALLS.

— *TERRY PALECHUK*

History and Development of Virginia Falls and Gorge

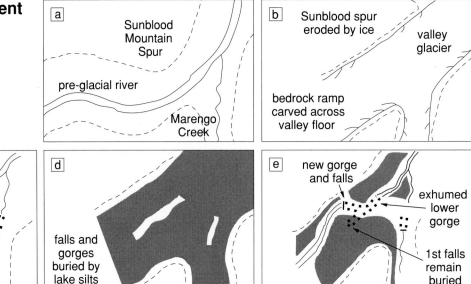

a Sunblood Mountain Spur

pre-glacial river

Marengo Creek

b Sunblood spur eroded by ice

valley glacier

bedrock ramp carved across valley floor

c 1st falls and gorge

(current portage trail)

d falls and gorges buried by lake silts

e new gorge and falls

exhumed lower gorge

1st falls remain buried

THE EVOLUTION OF VIRGINIA FALLS.

swimming across the river above the rapids. The calf was unable to fight the current and was washed through the rapids and over the falls.

During the lay-over, everyone found time to make use of the sunshower, our portable shower bag. When left full of water to warm in the sun or when filled with warm water from the stove, it yields a most satisfying luxury. Doubters are silenced when they learn that even the thickest and longest hair can be washed and rinsed from a single filling, with enough water remaining for a bald guy like me to get a good wash.

Later that day, during supper, the hikers reported that the view from the top of Sunblood had been worth all the sweat. From the alpine meadow on the summit, they could see the river they had already paddled and the stretch that lay ahead. The view unfolded for them another intriguing story of the Nahanni's geological history.

Originally the river missed this area altogether and followed the Irvine Creek Valley. When the river did move into the valley it now follows, a spur of Sunblood Mountain blocked the location where the falls now tumble, so the river followed the bed now occupied by Marengo Creek. After a valley glacier severed the Sunblood spur, the river began to flow over today's course, except that Fourth Canyon had not yet been eroded out. As the canyon was carved, the falls worked themselves back to where the current portage trail lies. Finally, extensive silting from the Glacial Lakes filled in that course, and the river began to follow the existing falls channel.

BILL MASON, FILM MAKER, ENVIRONMENTALIST, PAINTER, AND AUTHOR, ATOP SUNBLOOD MOUNTAIN ON HIS FAVOURITE NORTHERN RIVER.

— PAUL MASON

According to the park information, the falls are creeping upstream at a rate of four millimetres per year.

While we were sitting around the fire that evening, someone asked me how I had managed to become one of the few outfitters allowed to guide on the river. I explained that the story really went back to that first trip when I had met Father Mary in Deadmen Valley—the same trip on which we had encountered the prospectors. I told them my own story.

Chapter Seven

Dreams Unfold

Whiskey's for drinking and water is for fighting over.
— Mark Twain

That night in Deadmen Valley, on my first trip down the Nahanni, after the stories were finished and I was alone by the fire, a strong, warm, chinook wind began to blow in from the west. The twilit sky showed the tell-tale lenticular cloud or chinook arch, giving the illusion of a dome over the mountains to the west. I couldn't sleep. Surveying the beauty of Deadmen Valley from our camp, I reflected on Patterson's long-ago remarks about his nearby camp: "We were kings, lords of all we surveyed.". I was impassioned with everything I had experienced in this magnificent place. I would have to return ... more than once ... many times! The wheels were rolling in my mind and visions of the possibilities filled my head.

When at the age of 15 I received Dick Turner's book *Nahanni* from a family friend, who was to know that someday I would be completely swept away by the river? At the time it was only more fuel for the fire—a larger-than-life book about a fabled land. Maybe partly because of the book, I went on to study outdoor education in university and then established an outfitting and guiding business in Alberta.

Leaving the Nahanni years later after my first trip, I vowed I would be back soon. I had learned from the wardens that the park allowed only one canoe outfitter to operate on the river. This policy might as well have been carved in solid granite. Wally Schaber, who later became a good friend, had been running trips since the mid-seventies.

Perhaps one of my character flaws is my propensity for rising to challenges. I was already canoe outfitting in the foothills of the Alberta Rockies, but I couldn't sit easy with the knowledge that a monopoly existed for canoe outfitting on this grand river.

My chance to outfit on the Nahanni developed only two months later, but only after the rescue of a family and countless bureaucratic hurdles.

A group of my friends were keen on a September trip to the North. After shuttling our van to Blackstone Landing on the Liard River so that it would be waiting for us when we arrived by canoe, I was answering nature's call in the bush near the shoreline. It was early on a frosty morning and from out on the river I heard shouts for help. Rushing to the bank I saw an aluminum boat floating with the current in the middle of the voluminous flow. Aboard were a man, a woman, a little girl, and a new refrigerator, but no oars or paddles. I couldn't make out the exact cause of their distress, but it was clear they were frightened of the Beaver Dam Rapids that lay downstream. Their motor appeared inoperative.

Quickly I searched the campsite where I had planned to leave the van and found a couple

SPIDER'S WEB.

— DEB LADOUCER

who were camped in a tent. I woke them in a hurry, the husband followed me, and we grabbed a canoe and paddled out to the boat. Tying our painter to their boat we began the task of towing them out of the current and into shore. They had run out of gas the previous day on their way to their home in the village of Nahanni Butte, 25 kilometres upriver, and they had drifted through the night.

The process seemed to take forever. Finally and fortunately, we landed within striking distance of the homestead of Edwin and Sue Lindberg. I say "fortunately" because the family in the boat had been out all night and they were hypothermic, particularly the man, who had jumped out of the boat during the night in a vain attempt to ground it on a sand bar. Sue Lindberg is no greenhorn when it comes to fast work, and in no time she had the family secure and recovering in her cosy log home. My fellow rescuer and I were treated to a welcome feed of pancakes before returning to our respective endeavours. As I was leaving the cabin, the husband shook my hand and said, "Any time I can help you let me know!". "Thanks," I said, but my mind was on the upcoming Nahanni adventure and I doubted we would ever cross paths again.

I returned from that second Nahanni trip hopelessly enamoured with the river and more committed than ever to the challenge of obtaining an outfitting licence.

It's probably a good thing I didn't realize it then, but the Government of the Northwest Territories was besieged at that time by hundreds of requests for outfitting licences each year and had become very efficient at turning them away.

In my young and foolish way I set about to acquire a licence. I began with enquiries to the obvious departments, and after getting the run-around numerous times, I was finally given a prescribed set of hoops to jump through that I now realize were calculated to be unachievable.

Besides a long list of bureaucratic prerequisites, I had to obtain the permission of the local people in Nahanni Butte. With a population of 80 people, this Native community was understandably not known for its receptiveness to outsiders and their proposals. The bureaucrats would have stumped me except for the trump card that I didn't even realize I had at the time.

In a Christmas phone conversation with Father Mary, I enquired about the health of the family we had saved. He told me they were fine, and at that moment it dawned on me that they could be my emissaries to the community. I had forgotten the promise of a favour.

A radio-telephone call to the village on a winter's night set the stage. My friend suggested that if I came to the settlement he would be my ambassador. No promises—but he would help where he could.

My friend Morten Asfeldt, one of my guides in Alberta, was a licensed pilot. His father had a small aircraft in Fort McMurray, south of Lake Athabasca. Morten, his dad, and his brother Henrik were keen on an adventure and getting some flying hours, so we crammed into the tiny cockpit for the eight-hour flight. Judging by the weather I knew the flight would be bumpy.

The drugs I took to keep me from getting sick knocked me out immediately. When I woke up after a couple of hours I looked forward in the cockpit and the two men at the controls were slumped over—dead for all I knew. Fearing the worst I shouted, "Who's flying the plane?"

Shocked upright, the two wheeled around and I realized that one had been sleeping while the other was reading the map. The plane was on autopilot. Everything was under control. So much for nerves.

On the way to Nahanni Butte we dropped in to Fort Liard to visit Father Mary, who fed us and insisted we spend the night. The next day was Sunday when normally he would boat the 75 kilometres to Nahanni Butte for church. Instead, he hitched a ride with us the next morning. Upon landing in Nahanni Butte we thought it proper to accompany our guide to church. We entered the log chapel still in a daze from all the travelling. Feeling self conscious as strangers in a small community, we grabbed the first available pew. By the time we realized there was a men's and a women's side of the church and that we were on the women's, it was too late to save face. While suffering the curious, confused looks of the rest of the congregation, we pretended all was well, and then took the first opportunity to make our exit.

Later I met various community members with my friend from the river. They agreed to the granting of an outfitting licence provided that I made sure there was benefit to the community when possible. Later that same afternoon, we boarded the plane for the long flight home, this time stopping in Fort Smith to deliver the necessary documents to further the licensing process.

I now work closely with the government's "Travel Arctic" people, both in the Nahanni region and in Yellowknife. We have developed a strong working relationship and I appreciate what they do. They are a dedicated lot and have the best interests of tourism in the North at heart. Together with both Travel Arctic and the Nahanni National Park staff we are making great strides in the interest of both the park and the river.

Over a decade has passed since that night in Deadmen Valley when I decided my destiny. I would not trade the years for anything.

I finished my story as the fire died down, and the music of the falls soon had us all sawing logs.

Chapter Eight

CANYON WHITEWATER

The trick is not to rid your stomach of butterflies,
but to make them fly in formation.
— Unknown

It was now "portage day" and our first taste of white water. I tell the uninitiated portage is the French word for "painful toil."

Following a breakfast of pancakes and honeydew melon, we loaded the gear into the canoes for a short paddle to the portage trail. As we cautiously hugged the shore, it was clear that no one wished to tempt fate by capsizing so close to the brink of the falls, even though the current here was surprisingly slow. Just around the bend the river picked up speed vertically!

In the end we each made three carries over the portage trail. I had explained that each person need only take what they reasonably could and that we would just plug away until it was done. Secretly I was pleasantly surprised to see the portaging so efficiently executed. On the trips where we use rafts or our eight-person voyageur canoes, we actually bring extra staff to accommodate this process because we find that those groups are sometimes less able to manage heavy lifting.

Because of the permafrost below the surface, the portage trail had suffered serious erosion from very little use. Even hardy plants have a hard time regenerating over permafrost when trampled. The park's solution is a narrow boardwalk that covers the upper half of the trail. You can imagine, when walking the boardwalk with a load, how much more difficult the portage would be if you had to negotiate a kilometre-long quagmire like the trenches at Vimy Ridge each time you made a carry. I have heard the occasional "tsk! tsk!" in the city about the boardwalk, but I've never heard a negative comment at the bottom of the trail. Funny, eh?

We conducted the portage at a leisurely pace, passing around trek bars at intervals to sustain us until lunch. By 2:00 p.m. the sum total of our material possessions lay in a pile on the talus beach at the base of the trail. We stood more than half a kilometre from the base of the falls, but the spray was still noticeable, at first as a welcome cooling, and later as a call for warmer clothing so that we could enjoy lunch without shivering.

The falls divide around a large rock which the guides know as "Mason's Rock" after Bill Mason, a celebrated canoeist, environmentalist, film-maker, and artist. The highest side of the falls drops 89.9 metres; the low falls drop 52 metres. Because of the erosive action of the falls, which created Fourth Canyon, some day Mason's Rock may be a solitary spire standing downriver from the falls.

The numbering of the canyons on this stretch of river seems reversed at first. You have to remember that they were named before an aircraft had ever flown in the North. Anyone travelling

CANOES ON THE BEACH
BELOW THE CLIFFS OF
PAINTED CANYON.

— HENRY MADSEN

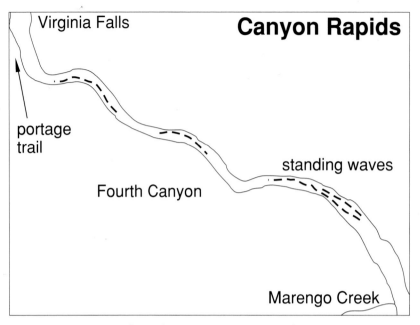

THE POSITIONS OF THE RAPIDS IN FOURTH CANYON, ALSO KNOWN AS PAINTED CANYON.

down the river would first have had to travel upstream. This canyon would have been the last one encountered.

Finally, after we had sacrificed many rolls of film to the falls, it was time to load the canoes and attach the spray decks. I passed on some final wisdom regarding the run through the canyon below. After a technique and safety discussion I suggested that everyone apologize to their partner beforehand for anything they may say in the heat of the moment. The rapids are not technically demanding, but the skilled judgement of an expert is necessary to discern the best line to take through them. Since the channel is deep there and there are few rocks to dodge, I told the group they'd be easily able to follow my line. Herb would be in the middle spot to lend guidance to those bringing up the rear.

Hollers, yahoos and even the occasional "Unreal, man!", mixed with other shouted and frenzied communications, took us from the maw of the canyon to the first bend without mishap. We pulled into an eddy so that the group could unpack cameras in the relative calm to capture the colours of the Painted Canyon—Fourth Canyon's other common name—before heading back into the waves. We took off again, each successive bend yielding yet another wild ride of rollercoaster waves and cries of, "This one is it!"

We all made it through the canyon right side up, as I had assured everyone we would, and then we stopped for a break at Marengo Creek. Away from the mist of the falls we felt suddenly hot and hurried to strip down layers of clothing that had seemed essential only minutes earlier.

Back on the river we encountered subdued waves until the False Canyon, a short-lived replay of the Painted Canyon. As the canoes pulled in, one after the other to an inviting, island campsite downstream, we were still talking excitedly.

The selection of a good campsite is paramount to evening comfort: a breezy spot to avoid mosquitoes, the requisite incredible view (for which everyone had come all this way), flat spots for tents, enough height to avoid flooding out, and secluded spots in which to hide the biffy and the shower. On this particular evening our esprit de corps was so high we could have been camped on the moon. I think that some of the group had been secretly surprised by their own nerve.

Tomorrow would be Hell's Gate. The group retired shortly after dessert and it wasn't long before I could hear rhythmic snoring.

As I sat by the campfire, I thought about the group behind us who would be arriving at Virginia Falls tomorrow. They were using our large ten-metre voyageur canoes which we had specifically designed for the Nahanni almost ten years earlier. The creation of these craft has been a highlight for us.

After our first year of outfitting on the river I became aware of the need for a new design of boat. Up until then, our guests could only choose between the traditional open Canadian canoe or an inflatable expedition raft. The canoe is such a big part of Canadian history and culture that, as Bill Mason pointed out to me once, it has a greater claim to the Canadian flag than the maple leaf. Lots of people who wanted to canoe the river didn't have the stamina for the small boats but wanted more participation than the raft would offer. I wanted to offer this group a chance to canoe.

Inspired by the large birch-bark fur-trade canoes of the voyageurs, Canada's early canoeists who freighted furs from across Rupert's Land to Hudson Bay, I began my research. Surely, if the voyageurs could build a canoe capable of crossing the continent loaded with furs and trade goods, we could build a similar canoe using modern materials. The crux of the problem, however, was that such a craft would have to be transported by small bush planes. How do you get a ten-metre canoe inside the six-metre cabin of a Twin Otter?

Before sinking the necessary money and time into the project, I wanted to be sure that a large canoe was suitable for the big river. There were no "sectionable" voyageur canoes available for the test, so I rule out flying upriver. As a solution I gathered together five unsuspecting but keen friends, and in the fall of 1985 we embarked upstream on the Liard River headed for the Nahanni. We had nothing but paddle power and the ambition of young and adventurous spirits.

Unsure of what lay ahead we pressed onwards, soon realizing that even in the slower current of fall we were better off pulling the canoe than paddling it. Five of us pulled from shore with a long rope while one person steered in the stern, keeping the bow away from the shore. This was a slow and tedious process. The rope snagged constantly on the myriad logs and rocks that covered the shore. The five on the line would each eagerly await their chance in the boat while the person in the stern slowly froze in the fall weather and anxiously awaited the switch to rope duty.

THE VOYAGEUR CANOE IN SEC-
TIONS OUTSIDE THE TWIN OTTER,
THEN STACKED AND PREPARED FOR
LOADING IN THE AIRCRAFT.

TOP:
— NEIL HARTLING

MIDDLE:
— HENRY MADSEN

FLOATING THROUGH THIRD
CANYON IN A 10 METRE
VOYAGEUR CANOE.

LARS, MY YOUNG APPRENTICE, SUPERVISING THE CUTTING OF ONE OF THE PROTOTYPE CANOES. IT REALLY HURTS TO BUILD A BEAUTIFUL BOAT AND THEN CUT IT INTO PIECES!

— *JUDY HARTLING*

THE "CONE HEADS," PORTAG-ING THE EARLIEST PROTOTYPE AROUND VIRGINIA FALLS.

— *BRAD ATCHISON*

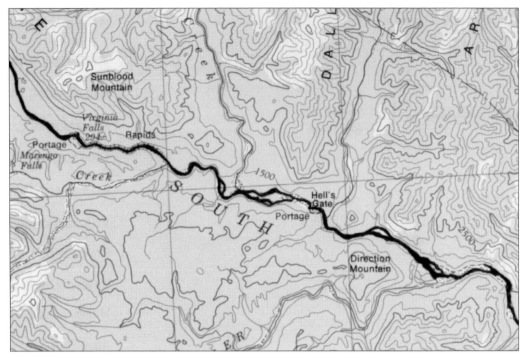

OUR ROUTE FROM VIRGINIA FALLS TO HELL'S GATE

On the rope you spent as much time in the water as on shore because of all the snags and brush tangles.

Along the Nahanni, by the last week of August, fall colours are showing, crimson and gold dominating the spectrum. Nights may dip down to freezing. Our September journey had the best of the vivid colours.

The days were long. Our progress was so painfully slow we were beginning to doubt our ability to reach Virginia Falls in the allotted time. After sleeping under the overturned canoe, we would be up by seven, breaking the ice off the water pails. Around eight, we were ready to embark, just as the sun was beginning to peek over the mountains. During the day, we allowed a 15-minute break to wolf down a bag of cookies and a half-hour stop for lunch. The rest of the time, we pulled. We selected our campsites around dusk. Supper and chores were by the light of our head-lamps and sleep came quickly each night.

Our group of six included Scott Fisher, an aspiring professional soccer player, Mary Coutts, an outdoor education student and mother of a 12-year-old son, and Ian Hosler, an outdoor camp director. The two remaining members —Brad Summers and Debbie Large—evoked mutual gleams in each other's eyes as we progressed. As we watched the romance from a distance, the rest of us would remark, "It's still a dangerous river!" They are married now and have a young family.

As we entered the canyons we were surprised to find our mileage improving. With the low autumn water level, the shoreline was relatively free of high-water debris. The greatest hindrances were the ever-present boulders, which tried our concentration and punished our feet. Alternately wading in thigh-deep water and clambering over the rocks destroyed one pair of footwear for each of us. We were able to identify with Patterson's description of the challenges and rewards of upriver travel in his book.

Twelve days of this upriver plodding finally placed us within striking distance of Virginia Falls. I will never forget the sense of exhilaration when, at dusk on the last possible day, we rounded the bend in the gorge to face the gargantuan falls.

The downriver paddle took two days.

When we got home, I consulted with canoe builders Mark Lund and Grant Heyden and we toyed with various design possibilities. Finally, after a winter of construction, my parent's garage gave birth to a pair of canoes, eight-metre prototypes of our voyageur canoe. Crafted of cedar strips sandwiched between layers of fibreglass, the canoes looked beautiful. The two pieces of each could be nested for loading into the aircraft and then bolted together with caulking compound in the seams when they reached the river. I endured many Noah's ark jokes and lots of scepticism about the sectional design of these large canoes, but the inaugural voyage was a success! In time we developed a strong reputation for this unique canoe in which almost anyone can enjoy the Nahanni canyons.

The years have seen improvements in design and materials. We have entered the space age and now employ plastics technology. We make the canoes from polyethylene, dramatically increasing their durability and functionality. To our knowledge, at just under eleven metres they are now the largest plastic canoes in the world. Manufacturing these boats has become a sideline.

Kirk Wipper, president of the Canadian Recreational Canoeing Association and founder of the Kanawa Museum of Canoes and Kayaks, renamed the Canadian Canoe Museum, in Peterborough, Ontario, has travelled the Nahanni in our voyageur canoes. A model of the innovative craft is displayed at the museum. As part of the planning for an international expedition, we even have one of the boats stored in the basement of the Chinese Sports Headquarters in

Beijing, China. My boat-building friend Wade Varonelli and I had to design that one to fit in the belly of a 747.

Over the years, the voyageur canoe trips from Virginia Falls have become one of the most popular ways to see the river. The Nahanni has been a source of inspiration to many people over that time, and it makes me happy to know that these canoes stand as another unique aspect of Nahanni history.

MEADOW OF YELLOW DRYAS
ON SECRET CREEK.

— MORTEN ASFELDT

Chapter Nine

THE DANGEROUS RIVER

*Gullibility is the key to all adventures. The green horn is the ultimate victor
in everything. It is he that gets the most out of life.*
— G.K. Chesterton

Sometime during the night the rain began. By now, the sixth night of our journey, everyone habitually weatherproofed their tent-site each night, making sure that everything was under cover in case of rain. Predictably, we were slow to rise when we heard the rain. Instead of stopping, the rain only increased in intensity. "A good day for more rapids," someone said. We ate a quick breakfast and soon we were riverbound.

Proper clothing is critical when you're on the river in such conditions. There are no substitutes for durable rain pants and a jacket. Sailing suits work perfectly. Those who hope to get by with so-called breathable waterproof fabrics are kidding themselves as much as those who try to cut corners with cheap plastic suits. Good footwear can also make the difference between enjoyment and misery. Tandem canoeists prefer neoprene wet-suit booties or rubber dry socks. Voyageur canoeists and rafters can be comfortable in regular rubber boots. Light hiking boots serve well for camp wear and hiking.

The confluence with Clearwater Creek came upon us quickly. With the low cloud hanging in the valley, this was the perfect setting for Albert Failles' story of Jorgenson, one of the Nahanni's puzzling mysteries. Albert had called it "Murder Creek." Martin Jorgenson built his cabin near here in 1912. His partner, Osias Meilleur, went out to Fort Simpson in the fall. They agreed to meet in Fort Simpson the following summer, but Jorgenson did not show up.

Meilleur later claimed he had learned from Indians that they had seen Jorgenson in 1913 travelling up the Flat River. Gus Kraus, a local trapper, adds that Jorgenson gave a note to a trapper named Jules to pass on to Billy Atkinson, Jorgenson's partner. This would have required an arduous trip upriver and over the Continental Divide. Jules gave the note to Mrs. Field, Billy's former wife, who passed it on to her new husband Poole Field. According to Patterson's book the note indicated that Jorgenson had found gold.

1914 found Meilleur back in the Nahanni. In the fall, he found a burned cabin where he and Jorgenson had built a cache in 1911. A loaded rifle, a revolver, and clothes lay in and around the ruin. Curiously, although he recognized Jorgenson's clothing, he did not report the find to the police. Nor did he report finding Jorgenson's body, which Poole Field found a year later at the same spot. Field had arrived in response to Jorgenson's note and was accompanied by Billy Atkinson and a man named Olaf Bredvic.

The RCMP recorded the death in 1916, after an investigation. Corporal Churchill and

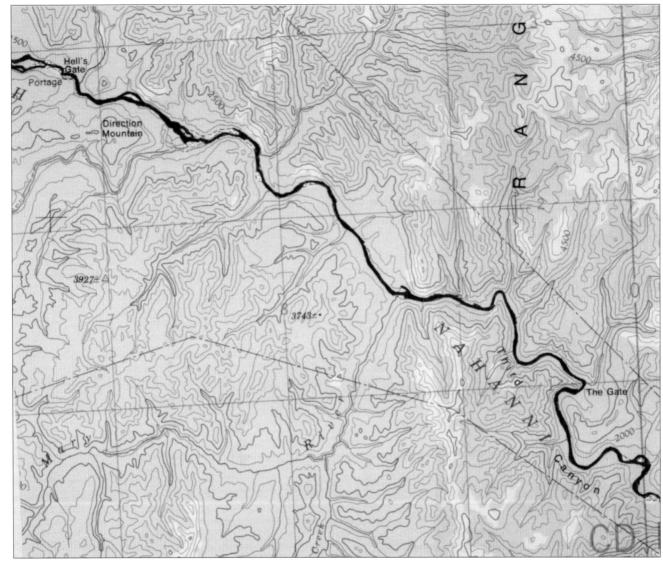

Our route from Hell's Gate to The Gate.

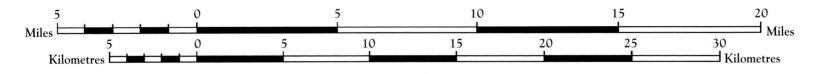

Special Constable Hope departed Fort Simpson on August 4th and arrived at the burned cabin on September 21st. They exhumed Jorgenson's remains for examination. In the end, they dropped the case because of the disturbance of evidence.

Once I stopped talking, we soon reached Hell's Gate, also called Figure Eight Rapids. Here we pulled over to scout the white water. A short trail takes one to a promontory overlooking the wildest portion. After some study, we plotted and agreed on a route. With a mixture of butterflies and knots in our stomachs we straggled back to the boats.

Our route took us alongside the largest waves and everyone agreed that although it was short-lived it had been the best white water so far. I silently mused at how much moxie this group of greenhorn canoeists had acquired in two days.

Soon we came to the confluence of the Nahanni and Flat Rivers. The search for gold earlier in the century was focused on the Flat. A tinkling sound could be heard on the bottoms of the canoes. I encouraged everyone to put their paddle grips to their ears with the blades in the water to amplify the noise. The water of both rivers is a finely formulated cutting slurry of clay, silt, and water. You can hear silt on your paddle anywhere, but here at the confluence the sediment is active enough to be heard on the bottom of the boat.

In time we came to Mary River where we often see mountain caribou. In 1921, up in the Flat River country Tu Negaa Dehé, May Lafferty, a young in-law of Poole Field, disappeared while hunting with Poole and his wife. Poole Field reported that she had been acting strangely for some time. Turner states that expert Native trackers were camped nearby and assisted a search. They included Diamond See, Boston Jack, Yohe, Tesou, and Big Charlie. The mosquitoes in the bush were fierce, and Lafferty's trail led a great distance over difficult terrain, including steep cliffs. The searchers eventually began to find discarded items of May's clothing, until she must have been naked. Finally, after nine days, the trackers gave up when the trail disappeared. May Creek was named in her memory. The Slavey name is Ts'elį Ets'ǫdéhtłah Dehé meaning "a little girl lost creek."

Mary River was named for Mary Kraus, who lived with her husband Gus at the hotsprings and had shown warm hospitality to a survey crew. The spot also signals the entrance to Third Canyon, a deep incision through the Funeral Range. Geologists tell us that the range was created by the lifting of strata between two fractures of the earth's crust called thrust faults.

Our goal for the day was to reach the Gate—not to be confused with Hell's Gate. Here the river narrows through a deep chasm within the Funeral Range.

The sky was clearing and the weather was improving as we approached one of my favourite illusions. Looking downriver we could see a puzzling sight. Apparently we were boxed in; the river seemed to disappear. To the left was a large hanging valley, straight ahead and to the right were the steep walls of Third Canyon. A creek rushed out of the valley, clearly indicating that it was not the course of the river. Puzzled looks spread across faces.

The current sped us towards the cliff and the answer to the puzzle. Suddenly a steep-walled abyss opened up to our right, punctuated on the left by the imposing bulk of Pulpit Rock.

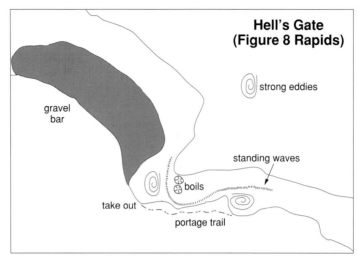

A MAP OF HELL'S GATE (FIGURE 8 RAPIDS).

We pulled into the boulder-strewn shore above the rocky stream, anxious to stretch our legs. We packed some lunch and prepared for a hike. A few were staying behind and would eat at the river's edge.

The trail we took led up the creek valley a short ways and then ascended the backside of the cliff above us. Before long we were scrambling through a boulder garden, exercising great care to avoid dislodging rocks. Occasionally a small one would slip out underfoot and the resounding call of "Rock!" warned those below to beware.

Looking out over the Creek Valley we could see that the river used to run in the creek valley, in opposition to the present gradient.

Swinging around the rock mass, it linked up with the today's route, completely avoiding the Gate, which at that time was solid rock.

Over the millennia a fissure must have opened, allowing some of the water to course through a shortcut in the canyon wall. Over time, the land lifted, elevating the meander. This quickened the erosion of the canyon passage, leaving a land bridge over the gap. Eventually the bridge collapsed, leaving the Gate in its present configuration.

In less than an hour we had climbed from the river to the top of the canyon. Third Canyon and a striking view of Pulpit Rock—dwarfed now by the magnitude of the surrounding cliffs—lay framed below us.

Our canoes were mere specks in the camera lens. It was another good day for the Kodak corporation.

We enjoyed lunch and I stretched out on the grass. The atmosphere below a good felt stetson, tilted over one's face and baking in the sun, is very conducive to sleep, particularly following

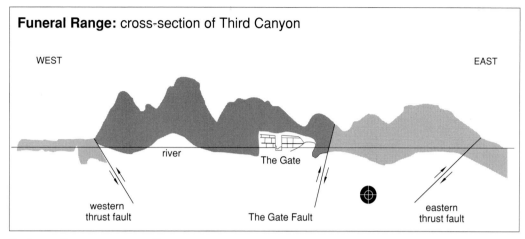

Funeral Range: cross-section of Third Canyon

WEST

EAST

river

The Gate

western
thrust fault

The Gate Fault

eastern
thrust fault

THE FUNERAL RANGE CONTAINING THE GATE WAS THRUST UPWARD AS A BLOCK.

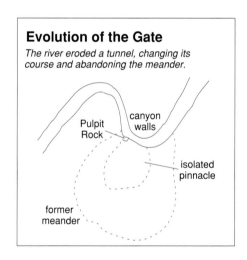

Evolution of the Gate

*The river eroded a tunnel, changing its
course and abandoning the meander.*

canyon
walls

Pulpit
Rock

isolated
pinnacle

former
meander

AT ONE TIME THE RIVER MEANDERED WIDELY UNTIL IT MADE A DRAMATIC
BREACH OF THE CANYON WALL, CREATING THE GATE.

a good lunch. I find myself falling victim to this phenomenon more often as the years pass. It wasn't long before I was studying the insides of my eyelids.

The descent took as long as the climb. Balancing from one rock to the next requires concentration and I heard more than one colourful description of the shortcomings of bifocals.

The float through the Gate inspired an attitude of reverence. Here the river is squeezed to half its usual width, with none of the characteristic waves that usually result from such a constriction, because the river gets significantly deeper at this spot.

For a guide, moments such as these make it all worthwhile. Few words are spoken; you hear only the intermittent sounds of camera shutters, water dripping from paddles lying across the gunnels, and voices breathing "unbelievable!" or "incredible!" The Nahanni works its magic. After the incredible bird's-eye view from the top of the Gate, the riverine perspective comes as icing on the cake.

Quietly we carried on to our camp. The canyon country breaths tranquil content as shadows fall.

After supper we sat draining the coffee pot and watching the fire turn to embers. Having put

Hell's Gate behind us I figured that it was safe to tell of an epic Figure Eight experience.

I know that at times my outdoor peers have accused me of having horseshoes in the right place when it comes to business matters. Like Stephen Leacock, the Canadian humorist, I believe in luck, and I find that the harder I work the more I have. I do recall one day, though, when I wasn't so lucky.

Ginger Gibson, Fritz Feldman, and I were working together guiding a private group in the voyageur canoes. No sooner had we landed at Rabbitkettle Lake than Fritz had a severe allergic reaction and had to be evacuated by aircraft, within an inch of his life. We thought, perhaps hoped, that nothing could go wrong after that—wishful thinking.

Ginger and I carried on down the river with our unique crew. Among the group were Euclid Herrie, CEO of the Canadian National Institute for the Blind, and himself totally blind. Also on board were Pat Guy (whose husband had been a judge of the Court of Appeal of Manitoba), a couple from Germany, a vice-president of a large financial institution, an American family, and several others. The average age of the group was about 65.

We left Virginia Falls unusually late in the day, mainly because of the loss of Fritz, on whose physical strength we had been counting. To top it off the weather was deteriorating. I made an omission that was to haunt me later on when I didn't insist on securely tying every last item into the canoe. We had a great time negotiating the Painted Canyon with our two big canoes and one raft. The large, stable voyageur canoes did their thing perfectly. Feeling cocky, I decided we would paddle Figure Eight Rapids before camping.

By now it was pouring rain, and as we approached the rapid I made a judgement call. Years of running the rapid without any difficulty were about to count against me. In my hurry I failed to detect a subtle change caused by the unusually low water level: there was not enough water to flush me through on our usual route. Because of my mistake—a lesson that could only be learned through trial and error—I was facing both trial and error at the same time, on a blustery evening.

As I lined up for the run with the usual manœuver, it looked routine. The large boat was managing the waves easily, but as we neared the rock wall I was struck by the lack of decisive turning that we normally derived from the current. Instead, we were thrust against the cushioning wave that rebounds from the wall and ended up recirculating in the upstream eddy. Not realizing the source of the problem, I thought that if we just tried a little harder we would be through.

So we tried the rapids again, this time pouring on the coal to round the bend in front of the rock wall, but the flow just wasn't there. Soon we were scraping along the wall and careening over a shallow-water ledge that sticks out from the cliff. I called for power from the paddlers and they responded instantly. At the same time, the hydraulic of the ledge swamped the stern of the canoe and ejected me, Pat Guy in the next seat, and sundry canoe packs into the flood. Euclid, the blind adventurer, was in front of us and oblivious to our absence. Still responding to my call for forward power they paddled the canoe clear into the big eddy at the bottom of the rapid before realizing I was gone!

I admit that, even from my river-surface view, I was smugly happy to see that in spite of

THE VIEW FROM THE TOP OF THE GATE.

— CAROLE CALENSO

everything, the canoe had safely delivered the remaining paddlers to shore—unpiloted! I was less pleased with my predicament. As I stroked madly amid the valuable flotsam, I found the vicious, cold current rapidly wisking Pat and me both out of sight of the others. Quickly, we teamed up, grabbing a floating pack between us and kicking for the near shore which would soon become the far shore if we let the current carry us to the next bend. Pat was a good swimmer. Conversing calmly, even joking, she confided that she would never have planned to spend her seventieth year in this way. I confided that, if I'd had my choice, I'd never have dunked someone who knew her way around a courtroom.

Luckily we made it to the target shore, although we were a kilometre or two below the rest of the group, cut off by a formidable cliff. With surprising efficiency we collected a flammable pile of tinder and firewood even in the wet weather. However, the cold water had taken its toll. My hands were so cold I couldn't bring my thumb and forefinger together to work the lighter. What a predicament! We persisted, knowing that we didn't have long to warm up before we would be in big trouble.

Fortunately a cool head prevailed upstream. Seeing the predicament, Ginger formulated a plan. Manning the raft with the most capable paddlers, she had the others prepare to portage around the rapids while she sped off to our aid. She had no idea how far I had gone or if I was even out of the river. I can't remember a sight that has brought me more relief than seeing that raft 'round the bend!

A flame applied to our fire pile created an instant blaze of inferno proportions. After we warmed up and secured the raft, we all scaled the bank and made the hike back through the bush to where the swamped canoe had landed—ironically, our intended campsite.

There was much rejoicing! We ate our spaghetti supper at midnight and retired to the tents, feeling peaceably content with life's simple pleasures. Much amusement was garnered from Euclids braille watch which had ceased running at 10:26.

The next day we were faced with the task of rounding up our river-borne items. Free-floating packs on the river seldom travel more that 20 kilometres before hanging up on a gravel bar or eddy. Watching carefully we made a contest of who would first spot the next item. When we pulled into our next camp we had retrieved the bulk of our losses. I'd learned my lesson.

In spite of the mishap we were back on track, pursuing our Nahanni dreams.

CANOEISTS LINGERING
BELOW PULPIT ROCK.

Chapter Ten

Deadmen Valley

There's gold, and it's haunting and haunting;
It's luring me on as of old;
Yet it isn't the gold that I'm wanting
So much as just finding the gold.
It's the great, big, broad land 'way up yonder,
It's the forests where silence has lease;
It's the beauty that thrills me with wonder,
It's the stillness that fills me with peace.
— Robert Service, *The Spell of the Yukon*

Morning brought another blue sky. The sun had already topped the rim-rock. The mountains to the west claim much of the air's moisture as it blows across, creating a near-desert climate and lots of blue sky. But mountain weather changes quickly. Travellers must be constantly prepared for downpours and strong winds, or for freezing temperatures at night.

Back on the river, the Big Bend loomed ahead. The gentle hairpin turn in the channel lies at the division of the Funeral Range and the Headless Range, and it demarcates Third and Second Canyons.

Soon we were weaving our way into the depths of Second Canyon. On river right, we saw Scow Creek a route for ambitious hikers to the heights of the Headless Range. The six-hour hike allows one to gaze ahead into Deadmen Valley and yields a wide-angle view of the river snaking through Second Canyon.

We chose an island just upstream of Headless Creek for camp. Herb and I got pizza sizzling in the ovens while someone else festooned the sandy beach with freshly done laundry. A steady chain of people took the shower bag around the corner to a secluded piece of beach.

After pizza and some homemade wine, I began my traditional reading for this spot on the brink of Deadmen Valley and in full sight of Headless Creek. The reading, from Raymond Pattersons's The Dangerous River, recounts the legends surrounding this infamous valley. Hands down, Patterson's eloquently written book is the best rendition of these tales.

We already knew of the grim fates of Jorgenson, May Lafferty, Mullholland, and Epler. The most significant remaining events surround the deaths of the McLeod brothers.

The story has many versions and conclusions. Patterson tells that Frank and Willie McLeod were the sons of Murdoch McLeod, the Hudson's Bay factor at Fort Liard. Spurred on by an Indian report of gold up the Flat River, the McLeods set out to the river in 1904 from Edmonton, a thousand kilometres to the south. From there they made a circuitous and bizarre expedition from Edmonton to Vancouver by train, up the coast by boat to Wrangell Island on the Alaska

A MORNING MIST HANGS OVER
DEADMEN VALLEY.

— D. SALAYKA

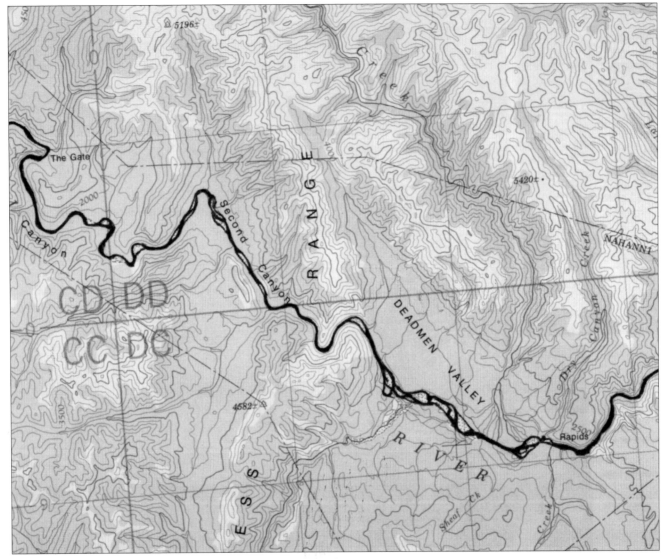

Our route from The Falls to Deadmen Valley.

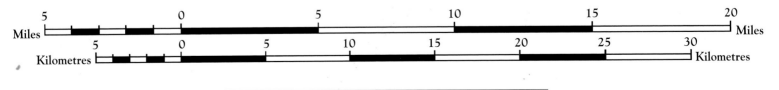

panhandle, and onto the frozen Stikine. With dogs and the primitive gear of the day, they travelled through the winter, 250 kilometres up the Stikine to Telegraph Creek, then on to Deese Lake and the Continental Divide. From there they pressed onward down the Deese River for 150 kilometres to the Liard River and then to another, smaller river which Patterson suggests was the Hyland. After another 250 kilometres they finally came to the upper Flat River, where they settled on a tributary of the Flat which they named Gold Creek. There they met Cassiar Indians who were sluicing three- and four-dollar nuggets. The boys were not as successful.

The placer mining technique involves sorting creek-bed gravels with a flow of water. When done properly, the heavier gold remains after the lighter gravel is washed away. The most productive device in the McLeod brothers' day was the sluice box, built from laboriously whip-sawed lumber. The open-ended box formed a long trough. Ridges nailed to the bottom aided in trapping the gold. Miners built dams on the creek to divert water through the box and then shovelled gravel into the upstream end. When the gravel was flushed through, the miners cleaned out and further panned the residue. Using a wide, shallow pan, they swirled the material with water to separate the fine sand from the gold particles.

Having collected what they could, the McLeods dismantled some of the Indians' sluice boxes and built a coffin-like boat. The McLeods got as far as the Cascade of the Thirteen Steps on the Flat, where they upset and lost nearly everything, save a rifle and some shells. Hiking the 30 kilometres back to Gold Creek they shot a moose, panned some more gold, built another boat and set out again. This time, they lowered their shaky boat through the rapids using a rope fashioned from the moose hide. Surprisingly, they survived their downriver run of the Nahanni and slogged through the upriver portion of the Liard to their home.

By today's standards, the rigours of the McLeods' exploit would be unimaginable. But after only one winter they were off again, this time taking the more direct route up the Nahanni. The story has it that a Scottish engineer by the name of Weir or Wilkinson was with them. An RCMP report of 1909 indicates that their provisions consisted of 50 pounds of flour, and five pounds of tea—meagre resources by any standards.

Nothing was seen of the brothers until 1908, when Charlie McLeod mounted a search and found his brothers' skeletons in their camp on the shores of the Nahanni in a broad unnamed valley. According to Patterson, G.M. McLeod, the boys' nephew, stated,

> *Charlie buried them without their heads. One brother was found lying in*
> *their night bed face up, and the other was lying face down, three steps away,*
> *with his arm outstretched in a vain attempt to reach his gun which was at the*
> *foot of a tree only another step from where he fell. The blankets were*
> *thrown half across his brother as if he'd left the bed with a leap.*

There were seven witnesses at the burial, and Charlie erected a cross over the grave. From that day on the area has been known as Deadmen Valley and the creek by the camp as Headless Creek.

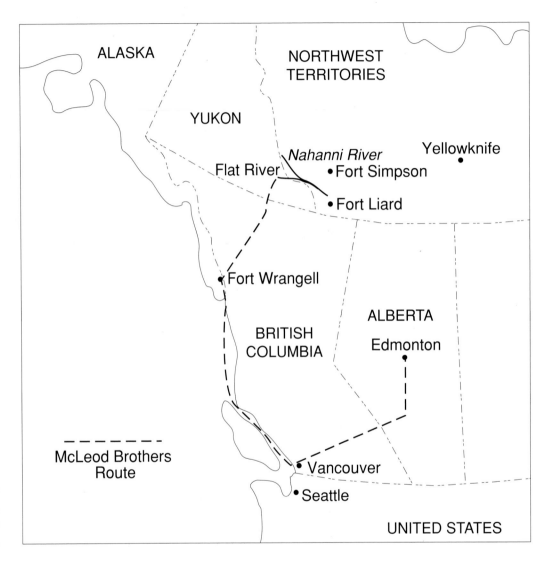

ALASKA

NORTHWEST
TERRITORIES

YUKON

Nahanni River

Flat River

• Fort Simpson

Yellowknife

• Fort Liard

• Fort Wrangell

ALBERTA

BRITISH
COLUMBIA

Edmonton

- - - - - -
McLeod Brothers
Route

• Vancouver

• Seattle

UNITED STATES

THE MCLEODS' FIRST JOURNEY
INTO THE FLAT RIVER AREA.
THEY CHOSE A CIRCUITOUS
ROUTE.

Not long after the burial, stories sprang up proposing answers to the mystery of the McLeods: what happened to their heads, their gold, and the Scottish engineer? Accounts ranged from believable crimes to tales of the supernatural. All of them received a great deal of attention and were repeated often.

To fuel the fire, the search party reported finding a split sled-runner in the death camp, upon which was written, "We have found a fine prospect."

The disappearance of the third man led to all kinds of suppositions. Patterson reports that some stories traced him to Telegraph Creek with a large amount of gold. Others said the RCMP followed his trail to Vancouver where he was supposed to have five thousand dollars' worth of gold. Poole Field tried to connect the incident to Jorgenson's fate.

The police reports tell a different story. They attributed the deaths to starvation and, although the case was reopened in 1921, there was no substantive evidence to contradict the original finding. The report doesn't mention the Scottish engineer.

As I told my subdued campers, the reality of corpses in the bush, human or otherwise, suggests there are natural explanations for the missing heads. Deadmen Valley has a healthy population of wildlife that would happily gnaw on a good set of bones, and there is no reason why they would confine themselves to one dining area. Indeed, the occasion of such a death would be a celebratory feast for a number of local species, and you can bet there would even be some resulting scrapping over choice bits. The consequences would be anything but an orderly presentation of remains.

But why let logic get in the way of a good story? The McLeod saga has fueled the imaginations of generations and, to a certain degree, protected the Nahanni from early exploitation. The fact remains that many of the Nahanni deaths have not been solved. What of the burned cabins, you ask? Wise travellers glance over their shoulders frequently.

We debated the possible conclusions around the fire until the last of us crawled into our tents.

Morning greeted us once again with the clear blue skies of a high-pressure system. Cornbread soaked in syrup was a breakfast hit. After ferrying directly across the river, we landed at the point where the Second Canyon wall peters out and meets the river. An unassuming dry creek bed makes an inviting gap in the bank. My friend Morten first pioneered this as a hiking route to the high country. When he suggested that it be named Morten Creek, I pointed out to him that if he wanted to put his own name on it he would also have to live with the small, barely perceptible promontory upstream being known as "Morten's Knob."

Our hike followed a dry, rocky stream bed, allowing us to circle up behind the Second Canyon ridge, to get an upstream view as well as a view of the imposing Tlogotsho Plateau, looming over Deadmen Valley.

Back on the river, we barely had time to wet our paddles before turning into the eddy created by Headless Creek. In homage to the lost prospectors we participated in another time-honoured tradition of the river. Forming a line, shoulder to shoulder with the cliffs of Second Canyon as a backdrop, we pulled our lifejackets up to cover our heads, perched our hats on top, and struck the "Headless Creek pose." After capturing the act on each camera for posterity, we decided that we too were in search of a gold of sorts, and could easily identify with the McLeod's quest.

Deadmen Valley is an expansive, mountain ringed area between First and Second Canyons. As you enter the valley from the canyon, the country suddenly opens up around you.

Soon to the north a peculiar spectacle came into view. The land appears as though it has

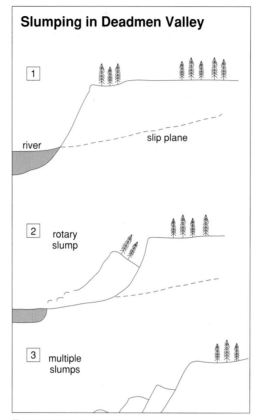

Slumping in Deadmen Valley

1

river   slip plane

2   rotary slump

3   multiple slumps

THE PROCESS OF LAND SLUMPING.

given up—as if it has given in to the river in one monumental stroke. A twisted jumble of trees witnesses the series of landslides that have occurred here. This spot is an example of "rotational slumping," which is caused by thawing of the permafrost. When the surface thaws, it collapses, leaving the ground unstable. Each slump exposes more of the ground to warming, leading to successive slides. Pat Wood, the inland waters supervisor in Fort Simpson, says that in the fall you can see from an aircraft that the river runs crystal clear until it reaches Deadmen Valley. At the slumps it picks up silt and runs brown from there on.

    Further down, on river right we passed Sheaf Creek—or, more correctly, Wheat Sheaf Creek—which was named by Raymond Patterson after an English Pub of the same name. With his partner Gordon Mathews, Patterson built a cabin here in the winter of 1928. Any remains of the cabin seem to have been claimed by the fire of 1981, which has certainly left its mark on the valley. Tall, fire-killed spruce stand to tell the story of the event. Fireweed carpets the hillsides

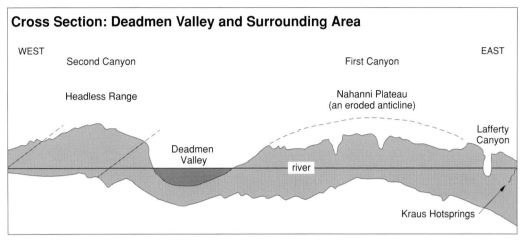

Cross Section: Deadmen Valley and Surrounding Area

WEST

Second Canyon

Headless Range

Deadmen Valley

river

EAST

First Canyon

Nahanni Plateau
(an eroded anticline)

Lafferty Canyon

Kraus Hotsprings

DEADMEN VALLEY IS ACTUALLY A SYNCLINE DISSECTED ALONG ITS EAST-WEST AXIS.

with hues of fuchsia. Fire is a natural event in the life cycle of the forest and allows a new generation of growth to be established. The park policy calls for no intervention unless the fire threatens people or buildings.

Dominating the horizon to the south is the Tlogotsho Plateau. Made of stronger sandstone than the surrounding country, the plateau is an expansive table-land overlooking the valley. Access to the tundra-like plateau requires a full day's rigourous hiking each way and you have to carry water. Tlogotsho means "big grass" in Slavey; the plateau is a major lambing area for Dall sheep.

Stomachs were grumbling by the time we pulled into the old Northwest Territories Lands and Forests cabin. Hailing from pre–National Park days, the log cabin was constructed in the early '60s. The location still holds a few attractions. A box on the porch of the cabin holds a registration book, a safety consideration to aid searchers in the event of a problem. Inside the cabin, along each wall and dangling from the rafters, are tiny, hand-carved paddles, each one representing a group that has passed through. Inscribed on each paddle are the date, the names of the group members, and often some bit of wisdom, a comment, or an inside joke. Our groups began the tradition ten years ago to counteract graffiti, which were beginning to show up.

Back in the bush behind the cabin lie the remains of a cabin built in 1945 by Natives who were apparently on their way to trap in the Yukon. Theirs was another woeful story.

The party was made up of Charlie and Jimmy Cholo, their wives, and four children under 12 years old, along with Alexis Mouse, his wife, their four children under 13 years old, 17-year-old Charlie Squirrel and 19-year-old Gabriel Gaszo. The expedition ended with the death of Mary Cholo, who was the victim of a love triangle. The case was tried in Fort Smith and several of the party were charged and convicted. Judge Baldwin described it at the time as the saddest case he had ever tried in the Northwest Territories.

While eating lunch in front of the old cabin, we gazed across at the expanse of Prairie Creek and its immense alluvial fan. The gravel fan spreads for four kilometres along the river shore and covers 15 square kilometres. This spot is known for strong afternoon winds and even small twisters, and today was no exception. Over the years I have chased tents, canoes, tarps, laundry, and all manner of expedition paraphernalia across the fan. I think the broad, flat expanse of gravel heats up in the afternoon sun, creating strong convection winds that in turn draw air out of the canyons. In cloudless conditions, radiant cooling during the evening often creates a valley mist.

Prairie Creek issues from its canyon at the upstream end of the fan. The canyon is robed in greens and fuchsia fireweed. The breach of Dry Canyon and the immense fracture of First Canyon lie downriver.

Herb taught us Dahtaehtth'ị, the local name for Deadmen Valley meaning "barren, wide-open area along the bend in the river." Kátadaatłah Dehé is the Slavey name for Prairie Creek and means "river of the clearing formed by forest fire." The depression of the valley is actually a syncline dissected along its east-west axis.

This valley was also host to another story, more recent than the McLeod saga. This more recent story elevated the romance of the Nahanni in the psyche of the nation.

BULL MOOSE FEEDING.

Chapter Eleven

THE LEGEND OF THE TWO PIERRES

*What sets a canoeing expedition apart is that it purifies you more rapidly and
inescapably than any other. Travel 1,000 miles by train and you are a
brute; pedal 500 miles on a bicycle and you remain basically a bourgeois;
paddle 100 miles in a canoe and you are already a child of nature.*
— Pierre Elliott Trudeau

In 1946 stories of the Headless Valley (a name that had come to refer to the entire Nahanni) by journalist George Murray surfaced in the Chicago Tribune and Toronto Star. On a continent that was seeking to replace the fervour of a world war, the story was a blockbuster. Nahanni became synonymous with unearthly phenomena. Stories sprang up in support of the reputation: tales of hidden tropical forests, murder, head hunters, hotsprings, canyons, waterfalls, and gold. Much of the reputation was based on fantasy, but an eager readership ate it up.

In short order, expeditions were mounted to this valley where it was said that 13 souls had perished. In 1947 a group of American marines planned a summer assault, while a syndicate of Canadians patriotically planned a March infiltration. The international race was on! Contenders from every corner of the continent lined up to announce their intentions.

Early in the new year, while the other expeditions were still on the planning board, the roaring piston engine of a Junkers aircraft rent the stillness of Deadmen Valley. The crew members were unknowingly ensuring the future preservation of the splendidly wild place into which they were intruding. On board was a young, enthusiastic journalist, seeking out material for serial newspaper stories, radio broadcasts, magazine articles, and pulp publications. Pierre Berton, destined to become a famous Canadian author, seized upon the legends of the lost prospectors, rekindling the old story and elevating the Nahanni in the consciousness of a young nation, bored and hungering for identity. With him were pilot Russ Baker, co-pilot and mechanic Ed Hanratty, and Art Jones, photographer for the Vancouver Sun.

Berton was no newcomer to the north. Hailing from the Klondike, he realized that the stories were implausible, but the lure was irresistible and the opportunity too great. Even his cynical, calculating editor, Hal Straight, was caught by the mania. Just before the flight, Straight took Berton aside and asked him to stake a claim for him.

Although it's a routine trip today, a winter flight into the Nahanni in '47 was a gutsy undertaking. They would be ski landing on a frozen river in an uninhabited mountain valley during the dark of January, hundreds of miles from assistance. Berton's two-week journey can be replicated with modern aircraft in less than 24 hours.

Developments on each leg of the foray were telegraphed back to the newsroom of the Sun.

FIRE-KILLED SPRUCE WATCH
OVER THE VALLEY.

— D. SALAYKA

THE JUNKERS ATF IN
DEADMEN VALLEY. ON THE
WING IS PILOT RUSS BAKER,
ON THE GROUND MECHANIC
ED HANRATTY, PIERRE
BURTON AND ART JONES.

— ART JONES

PIERRE BURTON (R) AND ART
JONES, SHORTLY AFTER LANDING.

— ART JONES

The syndicated story was burning up the wires across the nation. On the way to the Nahanni, the plane was pressed into duty for a mercy flight to Fort Simpson, evacuating a Native mother and child from Fort Liard. This heaped the coals on this hot story and the public ate it up.

The final staging for the upriver flight was at Jack LeFlair's cabin at Nahanni Butte. After overnighting in Jack's trading post, the crew had to thaw out the plane's engine with a blow-torch. Then it was off into the sky, over the river and canyons, on a bearing for Deadmen Valley.

Were it not for Baker's cool judgement, the group would have added another four souls to

PRIME MINISTER PIERRE ELLIOTT TRUDEAU AT VIRGINIA FALLS ON HIS TRIP IN 1970, THE YEAR BEFORE THE ESTABLISHMENT OF THE NATIONAL PARK.
— CANADIAN PRESS

the Valley's tally of dead men on that last leg. From the air, Baker saw that the river ice was rotten. Not wanting to give up, he circled the wind-swept valley to pick a landing area and finally chose the best of a bad lot. The plane was set for final approach. Seconds before touching down, Baker hit the throttle and the aircraft shot skywards, narrowly escaping a crash. At the last minute he had seen that what he thought was the shadow of the plane was actually shallow water running over a gravel shoal. Years of high pressure flying paid off once again.

Finally putting down near what was likely the mouth of Sheaf Creek, the little group spotted the remains of a cabin on the shore. Happy to be safely on the ground, they made their way

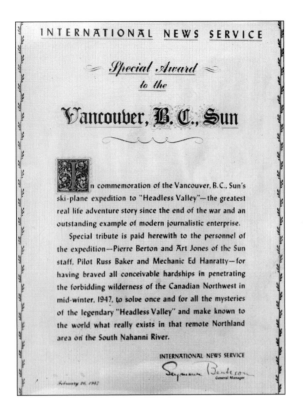

AWARD PRESENTED TO
BURTON AND JONES.

through the snow and photographed themselves, complete with a banner, beside the relic. "THE VANCOUVER SUN—FIRST INTO HEADLESS VALLEY" read the absurd sign, stretched above the historic cabin that likely belonged to Raymond Patterson.

In the eyes of the media, the race had been won.

A haunting wind howled down the valley, but the expeditionaries saw no indications of either head-hunters or gold. The fading winter light necessitated that they take off quickly. In the remaining daylight they followed an upriver course that took them on the sensational route over the remaining canyons and Virginia Falls, which was clothed in a shroud of ice. Just before turning back they could see the glow of the sun setting on the dramatic Ragged Range. They returned to the media world armed with enough stories to fuel Nahanni fever for a long time to come.

For Berton this trip was the birth of a personal industry. He identifies the flight to Nahanni as a turning point in his life. The river became his springboard into journalistic notoriety.

But the river benefited too. The Nahanni became an icon of Canadian wilderness, and people protect something they love.

This is a typical genesis of environmental protection. People will protect a legend, even if they have never seen it. Even the Junkers that made the Berton flight is protected. It is on display in the National Air Museum in Ottawa.

In 1959 an interdepartmental government study group recommended the Nahanni for national park status. Nothing came of this, and by the late 1960s the Nahanni was on the chopping block. The river had been surveyed for hydroelectric potential, and engineers were salivating over Virginia Falls and the canyons. Mineral claims were being staked in the area and major mines could not be far off. In those days, the prospect of a hydroelectric dam surrounded by a series of mines buying power was an attractive idea to the population in general.

Environmental groups fought the uphill battle to preserve the area. Gavin Henderson, a hard-working environmentalist, spearheaded the effort under the National and Provincial Parks

CARVED PADDLES ON THE WALL OF THE OLD NORTHWEST LANDS AND FORESTS CABIN IN DEADMEN VALLEY.
— WOLFGANG WEBER

Association (later to become the Canadian Parks and Wilderness Society).Despite their efforts, it became clear that if the Nahanni was to be saved, another event would have to vault it back into the public eye.

August 1970 brought the pivotal event in the fate of the Nahanni River. On a tour of northern communities, Prime Minister Pierre Elliott Trudeau decided to take a trip on the fabled river, to make up his own mind about whether Ottawa should permit the river to be developed. The canyons did not fail to work their magic. Once again the press began humming with "Nahanni." Returning to the nation's capital profoundly impressed, Trudeau encouraged his environment minister, Jean Cretien, to expedite the plans to protect the area as a National Park. This classic example of people protecting an area with which they have developed a relationship underscores one of the the important roles that guides and outfitters play in the process of ensuring that wild areas are protected. Our Outfitters Association has established the Nahanni Trust to raise money for future issues that may threaten the area. We also hope to have the park boundary extended to include upstream postions of the river.

Chapter Twelve

CANYON DREAMS

Adventure is not in the guidebook and beauty is not on the map.
Seek and yee shall find.
— From *On the Loose* by James Joyce

The mouth of First Canyon appeared as a dark void against the daylight. The Nahanni Plateau through which it slices is a major anticline.

After signing our freshly carved paddle and posting it in the Deadmen Valley cabin, we headed downriver floating towards the distant gap in the stone mass. We drifted past Dry Canyon Creek where a six-kilometre hike leads to a one-kilometre climb out of the canyon to the Nahanni Plateau. As we floated we scanned the slopes looking for the Dall sheep that frequent the mineral licks here. Our observing was rewarded by a group of ewes and yearlings that gazed at us from above. In *Horns in the High Country*, Andy Russell says, "Sheep may not be able to smell a dead horse, and may not hear thunder, but they can see through stone." These sheep were content to stand still and watch us, knowing that the distance between us secured their safety.

Soon we were in a widening of the river known as Patterson's Lake. It was here that Dr. Dave Larson, while guiding one of our trips, pulled into an eddy to assist a Labrador retriever that appeared to be lost. Doc got the surprise of his life when he realized that the dog he was about to pull into his canoe was a black bear! Both parties headed in opposite directions as quickly as they could paddle.

Guarding First Canyon is George's Riffle, an understated name if ever there was one. The rapid is named after George Sibbeston, who had a near miss there earlier in the century. We stopped on the island immediately above the rapid to scout a route. One at a time the canoes embarked, seeking out the pre-planned route. With great whooping and hollering from the paddlers, one by one the boats emerged into the quieter water.

Looking around I saw a rocky ledge just above the water and was reminded of the time I had made it through the rapids and was passing just beside the ledge. Lying there on his side was a big black bear, curled around a Dall sheep carcass. I think we were equally surprised. As I appeared the bear had one of his front feet in the air, doing something bearish. Upon seeing me he dropped his paw onto the sheep remains. The leverage of the heavy paw on the bones made them pop up and bop him on the nose, but he seemed to take no notice of his own comedy. In the instant it took for me to drift out of his personal space he raised his nose in the air and swivelled his head in an attitude that was clearly meant to indicate indifference.

While remembering this event I nearly forgot that our campsite was coming up. Just ahead was one of my favourite places in the universe. A broad, sandy beach that stretches for almost

LIVING OUT SOME NAHANNI DREAMS VIA THE VOYAGEUR CANOE.

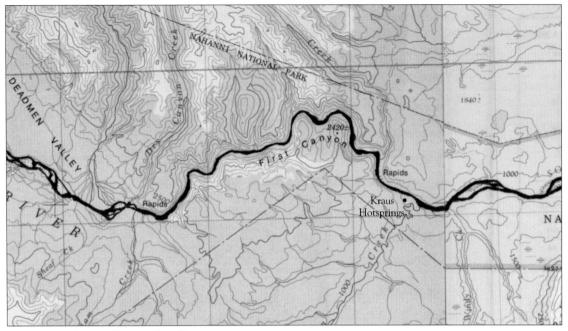

OUR ROUTE FROM DEADMEN VALLEY TO KRAUS HOTSPRINGS.

two kilometres, backed by tall cottonwoods and spruce, flecked by an abundance of driftwood, all in the shadow of cathedral-like cliffs. Rain or shine it is a majestic spot. Clouds passing among the mountain palisades seem to unite earth and sky.

First Canyon, named by Poole Field in about 1907, is the steepest and deepest of all the canyons. At over a thousand meters in height it stands as one of the deepest river canyons on the continent. The predominance of the harder dolomite rock has allowed the walls to remain steep and to erode less than the canyons upriver. Camping in the depths of the canyon is a humbling experience. The walls, soaring overhead, close out the sky and seem capable of folding you into the earth. The strata of the walls flaunt hundreds of thousands of years of earth history.

Unlike most younger mountain rivers the Nahanni does not cut a narrow straight course. Before the formation of the mountains, the Nahanni was a river of the flat plain, meandering in broad sweeps as a prairie river does. As the Mackenzie Mountains rose, the river cut across the grain of the land. The earth actually rose while the river held its own against the change. This process took place over roughly 1.4 million years.

A practical analogy is to liken the land to a plate of butter. Most younger mountain rivers are similar to a hot knife cutting down through the butter while the Nahanni is like the butter lifting up around the hot knife. Since it preceded the mountains, the Nahanni is called an antecedent river.

In spite of its meandering, the Nahanni is attempting to straighten the canyon, and to some extent it is succeeding. The heights of the canyon display this evolution graphically. Overhead, we could see the remains of two abandoned meanders, former twisting channels that gradually rose above the river.

"These cliffs sure do block out the scenery," someone said. Chuckles followed.

Springtime in the canyons is a dynamic time of change. The voluminous freshet of melt-water gushes through every crack and cranny. This lubrication between rock layers allows slip-page of rock pieces, some of which have been fractured through freezing action during the winter. A subdued replay sometimes occurs in the summer during rare periods of intense rain so the river traveller is well advised to watch for falling rock at these times.

From our sandy beach we watched the oscillating surface of the river. One would expect a mountain river with the Nahanni's gradient to have much more turbulence. This calm is accounted for by the history of Glacial Lakes Nahanni and Tetcella, created when the down-stream end of the river was blocked by Laurentide ice. In First Canyon, Glacial Lake Nahanni was more than 360 metres deep. The smaller Glacial Lake Tetcella was 200 metres deep. The Nahanni has not yet eroded the deposits of silt and clay left by the lakes to the original bedrock. Hence the river has a relatively smooth bottom.

Night in First Canyon came decidedly early as the arc of the sun was intercepted by the rim-rock. As the sun rose in the morning, the light crept slowly down the canyon walls, pushing the shadows into the river. Our necks were craned, studying the heights, as we embarked on the river that morning.

It is sacrilegious to do anything but float through First Canyon. This—the inner sanctum of the Nahanni—must be savoured; you are compelled to reverently regard the visual splendour that unfolds at every turn. Pillars, flying buttresses, turrets, spires, and ramparts give a heraldic appearance to the convoluted, twisting walls. The black and grey stone is mostly devoid of trees except for the occasional black spruce that clings tenaciously to a fragile niche.

The canyon environment is a cacophony of sound. The softest wind roars around pinnacles and in and out of crevasses. Irregularities and rock ledges along the shore make the sounds of rapids, even where the main channel is flat.

House-sized rocks in the river have apparently broken off the canyon wall above. During a hard, several-days' rain you can hear rocks falling in the canyon.

At the base of a striking massif, White Spray Springs issues forth. Crystal clear and frosty

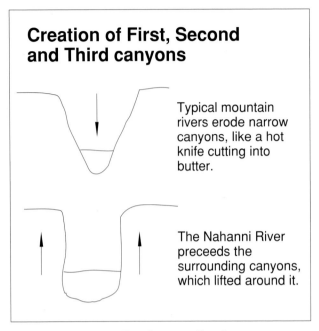

Creation of First, Second and Third canyons

Typical mountain rivers erode narrow canyons, like a hot knife cutting into butter.

The Nahanni River preceeds the surrounding canyons, which lifted around it.

DIAGRAM OF THE CREATION OF FIRST, SECOND AND THIRD CANYONS.

cold, the spring feeds a small creek as it gushes powerfully out of the rock. Its waters are so frigid that they create a cool downstream wind in the gulley. While this is a pretty spot and a good place to tank up on fresh water, it also provides a geological clue to the nature of the karst and pseudokarst phenomena of this area. The features above us here on the Nahanni plateau are the best examples of karst landforms in North America, and White Spray Springs drains the southern portion of the Nahanni Plateau. Up ahead at Lafferty Creek we would be able to see a graphic depiction of the karst story.

Lafferty Creek and the major side canyon of the same name lay immediately around the bend from the springs. It was named after Jonas Lafferty, who was prospecting in the area in 1922. Its Dene name Tthecho Dehé means "big rock river."

Jean Poirel discovered extensive caves high on the walls of First Canyon and Lafferty Creek Canyon in 1970. Since then over 200 cave entrances have been mapped in the area. One hundred and twenty are on walls of First Canyon. Most of them are plugged with ice and silt, but three have been explored to depths of more than a kilometre. The most famous of these is Grotte Valerie. Extending 430 metres north into the canyon wall, it lies from 40 to 60 metres below the plateau. There are over two kilometres of passages with three entrances. Grotte Valerie is a pheatic cave, which means that it was formed beneath the original water table (it would be

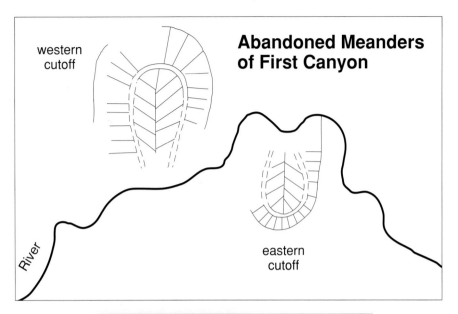

Abandoned Meanders of First Canyon

western cutoff

eastern cutoff

River

THE NAHANNI SHORTENED ITS COURSE THROUGH FIRST CANYON BY CUTTING THROUGH TWO MAJOR MEANDERS WHICH ARE NOW DRY AND ELEVATED ABOVE THE CURRENT RIVER LEVEL.

CANOEISTS NEGOTIATING GEORGES RIFFLE.

— *TERRY PALECHUK*

termed "vadose" if it had been formed above the water table). As is typical of karst formations, its walls and roof are well rounded and its passages are full of twists and contortions. Evidence of flooding by Glacial Lakes Nahanni is seen in the silt that covers the floor. Stalactites that have been dated older than 350 thousand years are growing on the sediment. They predate the last major ice advance, and therefore aid in piecing together a long sequence of geological events.

We could see the cave entrances from our position down below.

The original discoverers of these caves were met by the startling spectre of about a hundred Dall sheep skeletons, dating back over ten thousand years. The remains lie located at the bottom of an icefall within the cave. The sheep probably wandered into the cave over the years, slid down the ice, and were unable to escape back up the slippery incline.

The interior environment of the caves is delicate. Frost crystals adorning the walls can be damaged even by body heat. The ice under which the skeletons lie can be easily clouded by footprints. Due to this fragility, the caves have been closed to the public. This is easily enforced because of the precarious locations of the entrances. Technical climbing skills or a helicopter are required to get in.

FISHING AT WHITE SPRAY
SPRINGS. THE NAHANNI IS
HOME TO ARCTIC GRAYLING,
DOLLEY VARDEN, LAKE TROUT
AND NORTHERN PIKE. CATCH-
AND-RELEASE IS STRONGLY
ENCOURAGED.

— *TERRY PALECHUK*

Lafferty Creek offers one of the most direct routes from the river to the Nahanni Plateau and its karst lands. Still, it takes a multi-day hike to reach the top. Here above the tree line, the vistas are stupendous. We hiked up the creek for two hours, admiring the sculpted rock and the Lafferty Creek erratics: greenstone and other igneous rocks which came from the Canadian shield 250 kilometres east. The rocks were likely carried here by one of the early ice masses.

Hundreds of sinkholes puncture the top of the plateau. These natural culverts are created by the dissolving of the limestone by water. Rock towers, natural bridges, and eight major dry canyons provide dramatic evidence of the past action of water on the rock. Again, thanks to the lack of glaciation, these features have survived the ages.

Pat and Rosemarie Keough have explored the karst lands extensively. They report that the most unusual features on the plateau are karst streets and polges. The streets are long deep corridors that go as far as nine kilometres. Polges are large basins created by the dissolving process. The Nahanni Plateau has the most northerly polges in the world. Water in the polges is drained through sinkholes called ponors. A lake forms if persistent rains fill the polge faster than the ponors can drain. These lakes come and go throughout the summer.

The outwash of Lafferty Creek creates a rapid just downstream. If the breeze is upriver you can catch the sulphur odour of Tułetsee (literally smelly water)–Kraus Hotsprings wafting in the air. River travellers revel in these natural hotsprings at the termination of First Canyon. Lying in the pool by the river, we gazed into the canyon, recounting tales of upriver exploits.

THE SAND BLOWOUTS ARE A
SANDSTONE FORMATION
ERODED BY STRONG WINDS
FUNNELLED THROUGH THE
MOUNTAINS. THEY MAY BE
VIEWED THROUGH BINOCULARS
FROM THE SPLITS. ACCESS ON
FOOT INVOLVES FOREBODING
SWAMPS AND MUSKEG.

— *WOLFGANG WEBER*

Chapter Thirteen

THE SPLITS

*I would rather be ashes than dust! I would rather that my spark should burn
out in a brilliant blaze than it should be stifled by dryrot. I would rather be a
superb meteor, every atom of me in the magnificent glow, than a sleepy and
permanent planet. The proper function of man is to live, not to exist. I shall
not waste my days in trying to prolong them. I shall use my time.*
— Jack London, *Tales of Adventure*

When I soak in Tudetsi — Kraus Hotsprings, my mind is never far from the memory of Gus
Kraus, who in 1940 moved here with his wife Mary. Over the years, until 1971, they lived here
off and on with their son Mickey, prospecting, trapping, and gardening. The long hours of summer daylight combined with the warming influence of the hotsprings creates the perfect green-
house environment. The abundance of wild parsnips now found at the hotsprings is a legacy of
the Kraus garden.

The Krauses built a picturesque cabin at this spot, and in the northern winter one could
comfortably walk around inside without footwear.

Gus talked of the time he visited with Prime Minister Trudeau at the hotsprings. Soon after,
when the park was coming into being in 1971, Gus decided to move to Little Doctor Lake. The
new home was situated in a spectacular gap in the Nahanni Range.

Gus left Chicago in 1916 and worked his way north. He arrived in the Nahanni area in
1934. I once asked him if he had ever had any harrowing experiences in the area. He thought
hard and proceeded to tell me about the time he was walking a high ridge when suddenly an
eagle dived on him and grabbed his hat. An amusing tale, but hardly what I had hoped for. The
story did reveal two things about his nature.

First, to his credit, Gus was a very cautious man. One of the reasons he lived to the age of 94
when many of his contemporaries succumbed to the Nahanni was that he didn't tempt fate. As
the saying goes, "There are old river men and bold river men—but no old, bold river men."

Second, the story revealed his modest ways. I happen to know, as does everyone in the area,
that he had once been shot in the head. The circumstances were compromising to the two people involved, so by custom the full details are reserved for confidential discussion on the river.

Until his death in 1992 he was lively and cared for those around him. Mary and Mickey live
in the area still.

As we left the hotsprings, I reminisced about the time we found a man stranded below a cliff
downstream of the hotsprings. Only ten minutes after leaving the hotsprings, our attention was
caught by a waving white shirt on the shore. When we paddled over to investigate, we were

SOAKING IN KRAUS
HOTSPRINGS, RECOUNTING
TALES OF UPRIVER ADVENTURES.

— *TERRY PALECHUK*

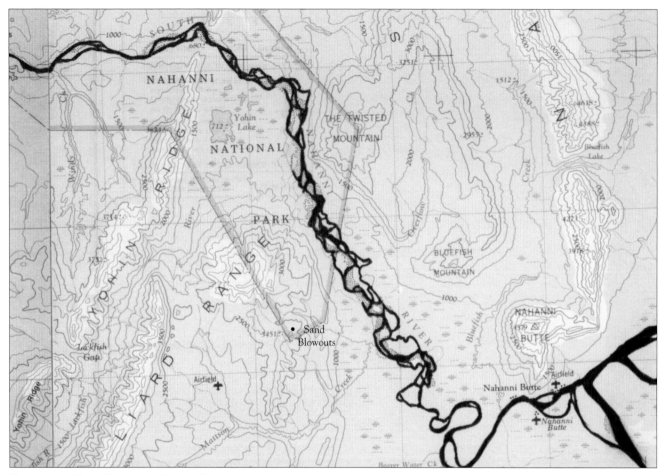

OUR ROUTE FROM KRAUS HOTSPRINGS TO NAHANNI BUTTE.

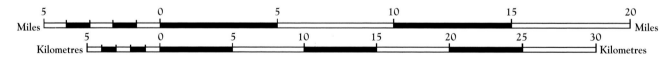

greeted by a survivor who was happy to see us. He introduced himself as Tom Collins. A week earlier he had embarked on a classic adventure, recreating Patterson's 1927 exploration by pulling his canoe upriver from the Liard. He had made good progress until he passed under a leaning tree. An errant twig poked his eye. Instantly, the tracking line was out of his hands and he was left with little more than his injury and some matches. High cliffs cut off both the upstream and downstream shorelines. Not wanting to leave the shoreline where he might be spotted by a passing group, he ruled out the possibility of bushwhacking around the cliffs. He stayed calm, made a camp around a fire, and sat there patiently for three days.

By the time we arrived he was beginning to wonder if he would ever be found. We were happy to give him a lift. We carried on down the river with one more person in the group.

In camp that night we pooled together extra clothing and made sleeping arrangements for Tom. He seemed reluctant to sit down and relax. Finally I sauntered over and suggested that he take a load off his feet. At first he brushed off the suggestion, then quietly he confided that he had burnt the back of his legs while lying in front of his survival fire, keeping warm. After some persuasion I got him to agree to let me look at the injury. In the privacy of a tent he bared the spot and I nearly fell over. Two deep burns testified to his stoic strength as well as his patience. I applied some dressings and nothing more was said of the injury.

As a kind thank-you, Tom later sent a letter to the editor of our local newspaper, publicly commending our group for "elevating his estimation of mankind."

After leaving the canyons, the river enters a region known as the Splits. This is the concise translation of the name Ndu Tah. Here, gravelly islands braid the channel. With the thoroughness of a scalpel the current carves away the bank here yielding the inner workings of the forest. The process of erosion is so persistent that the woodland has no chance to adapt and fill in its exposed ecotome with the usual protective understorey. The trunks of the aspen show pale white, like the skin under a bathing suit.

The Splits are also notable for their multitude of sweepers. They demand respect. The incising current has eroded the bank, encouraging trees to gradually topple into the river. Day-dreaming in the Splits is ill advised.

On one occasion in the Splits, I spent two hours perched on logs in midstream in the midst of a downpour, freeing a canoe. An elaborate pulley system finally worked, but the situation taxed our rescue repertoire and reinforced the old lesson that you can never let down your guard on a river regardless of the seeming lack of hazard. Northern mountain rivers demand consistent respect that southern paddlers sometimes fail to render.

The Twisted Mountain, named for tortuously folded strata, watches over the Splits. The Dene know it as Kandajoh meaning "something big pushing up, emerging." The original English name was O'Brien Mountain after trapper John O'Brien who froze to death in 1922.

The river runs through a gap between the trailing ridge of Twisted Mountain and the bulk of Mattson Mountain. It was here that the Laurentide ice dammed the river creating the glacial lakes.

An interesting phenomenon evolved from the lake formations. The glacier that blocked the valley had picked up boulders as it moved west over the land. Pieces of ice periodically broke off and floated as ice bergs on the lake waters. Some of these bergs contained rocks, and as the berg melted the rocks dropped to the lake bottom. These "drop rocks" were deposited throughout the valley.

Further on, the very southeast corner of Mattson Mountain exhibits lateral scouring by the ice. A large, lateral moraine can be seen on the north slope of the mountain. Training the binoculars another two kilometres south reveals a rock glacier. Below this field of rock lie the remains of a glacier.

In one of the big bends in the Splits the river widens and shallows out. The resulting snags and deadheads form a benign-looking but perilous trap: The Devil's Hole. You need some skill in current reading to navigate past the threatening logs. While navigating the Splits it's easy to relate to Mark Twain's accounts of piloting river boats on the Mississippi.

A predictable pattern seems to emerge over the days when I'm guiding a group. Mornings on the water seem to be dominated by chatter. People might be working things out with a new partner, telling jokes and stories, or discussing everything from relationships to politics. During post-lunch lethargy the airwaves are more quiet, but this is when questions are asked. I am often asked about the inner workings of the outfitting business. As we paddled the Splits this time, my paddling partner expressed her surprise at the multitude of arrangements required for our trip. She was amazed at the costs that appeared to be involved.

A journey on the Nahanni is an expensive proposition. Since we operate in a remote area with such a short season, the costs are high. In order to provide a consistently good experience we must plan more than a year in advance. We have to ship and maintain tonnes of equipment and supplies. Our staff must be trained and certified. Professional guides have to be paid and they too have to be transported and looked after. Anyone who lives in the North will tell you how expensive it is just to exist.

Our largest single cost is the upriver flights. Maintaining a million-dollar aircraft in a remote outpost is no easy task. They are held to the same stringent regulations as any southern flying service, yet the cost of fuel, pilots, engineers, parts, freight and office overhead are much higher here than in southern locations. Luckily for me, once they see the Nahanni, few people object to the cost.

The river had widened and was beginning to slow down.

Chapter Fourteen

NAHANNI BUTTE

*I left the woods for as good a reason as I went there. Perhaps it seemed to
me that I had several more lives to live and could not spare any more for that
one. It is remarkable how easily and insensibly we fall into a particular route
and make a beaten track for ourselves.*
— Henry David Thoreau, *Walden*

The Splits gave way to huge, sweeping meanders. On the horizon we could see the striking, bell-shaped silhouette of Nahanni Butte. In Slavey it is Ttenago: "the pointed rock." Such are the meanders that the Butte seemingly circles your position, as you paddle downriver. The map reveals that at times we are frustratingly close to the next bend over land, but following the river's snaking course seems to take ages. So near, and yet so far!

On the last long straight stretch approaching the Butte I perceive an atmosphere of resistance. In two weeks we had become friends with the river, and with each other. The thought of some fragment of civilization, regardless how small, caused something to recoil inside. The mood seemed detached, pensive, with the boats strewn across the river.

I was scribbling a page of my ongoing letter to my wife Judy. She has a career as a Crown prosecutor and consequently can't join me for many of these trips.

Since she's an avid mountaineer and skier, she sometimes feels hoodwinked in her choice of a spouse. Sure we share a love of the outdoors, but for much of the year that's as far as it goes. While I'm away on the rivers for weeks at a time, she can only make weekend trips. In the winter, my major promotional events are inevitably scheduled over weekends, which are the only times she can get away from work.

Since I have more than 30 staff and all the usual responsibilities of a business, winter is actually busier than the summer for me, so much of the time Judy is truly an outfitter's widow. Lars, my son and four-year-old apprentice, looks forward to the time when he is old enough to accompany his dad on these rivers. Jennifer and Jason, my stepchildren, are grown up now but they too have had to tolerate the idiosyncrasies of the outfitting business.

As we rounded the bend at the rocky base of Nahanni Butte, we could hear the community's diesel power generator. Soon the buildings of the village swung into view. Although pretty rustic, they looked out of place after our time away from architecture.

After landing immediately upstream of the settlement, we secured our canoes at a small campsite the villagers had built. Herb slipped away to visit his mother. The community of Nahanni Butte, as always, turned out to be far less intimidating than we felt it might be as we came off the river. It has a population of about 90 people who attempt to remain close to the

THE THREE BEARS.
AN UNUSUAL DISPLAY OF
BLACK BEAR TRIPLETS.

— *D. SALAYKA*

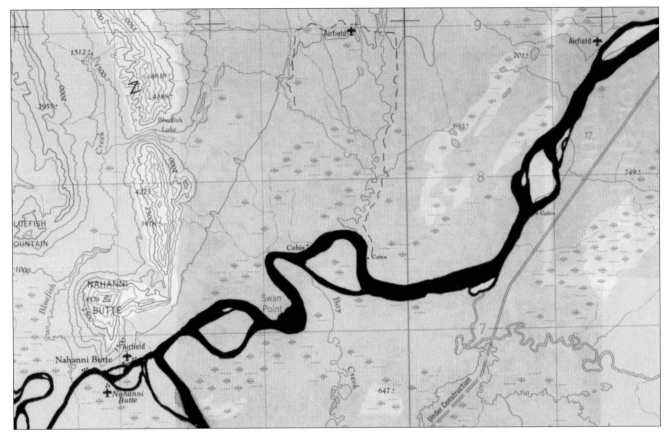

OUR ROUTE FROM NAHANNI BUTTE TO LINDBERG'S LANDING.

land. We didn't stay long among the cluster of cabins. We felt that we were peering into the quiet lives of a close community like the water incising the bank upriver; we were walking a fine line between visiting and violating their privacy.

We saw the village's children in the yards, playing with the enthusiasm common to all youngsters. They were curious about us and their toothy grins reached out to us. I hoped to myself that some of them would be future emissaries of the river in the way that Herb is. We have very few candidates like him. The world of urban adventure travellers remains very different from that of most Dene. For example, guides like Herb must prepare meals that are unheard of in these communities, assume roles that are not traditional to their gender, and undertake activities that may not make sense to them. One of our Native apprentices confided to me one time that he could not see the sense in hiking to the top of a ridge if you were not hunting a moose. We are working to introduce interested adult community members to guiding but my greatest hope lies in those toothy grins of the youngsters.

After reporting to the small park station in the village we made our way back to the campsite.

In Nahanni Butte on a late July night several years ago, Morten and two other guides—Les Parsons and Kathy Elliot—performed a risky rescue, saving the lives of a father and son. It was around 3:00 a.m. and darkness had set in briefly. The guides awoke to faint screams from the river. They set out with two canoes in the blackness, and it took them 15 minutes to race to the scene. In the light of their head-lamps, they found a father and his young son clinging to the bow of a boat that was standing on end, its motor sunk in the sand of the river bottom. Both were very hypothermic and dangerous to approach, since they could have tipped a canoe in desperation to climb in. The guides managed to get them aboard and paddled upriver to camp where there was a fire awaiting with warm drinks and dry clothes. They had been in the water for nearly two hours. Since they were wearing jeans and heavy jackets with no lifejackets, swimming to shore had not been an option. Both were very grateful. They knew it was a fluke that their screams were heard at that time of night, and they knew they had faced death. Throughout the rescue, the father repeated to his son how much he loved him.

The only record of the event was in the expedition log book, and if not for that I might never have heard of it. Just another night on the job.

Three things are certain in life: taxes, death, and mosquitoes in Nahanni Butte. Everyone put on their bug jackets or slathered on repellent. The settlement sits in the midst of the best mosquito lowlands possible. We realized now how fortunate we had been upriver. As a general rule you can avoid mosquitoes altogether on the upper Nahanni but here you must brace yourself.

We set about organizing camp for the night. Had we arrived here with the voyageur canoes or rafts, we would have been met by the Twin Otter and whisked back to Fort Simpson for showers and a farewell meal. Our practice with the tandem canoes, however, is to camp here and then carry on in the morning. Along with the Nahanni we merge with the mighty Liard River and continue the remaining 25 kilometres to Blackstone Landing, and Edwin and Sue Lindberg's homestead. We planned to get on the Liard early in the day to avoid the upstream winds that can render the river unnavigable in the afternoon.

Paddling in the shadow of Nahanni Butte, I am most cognizant of the Dene people and their history in this region.

Nick Sibbeston, the former Government Leader of the Northwest Territories is a Dene. In

WOOD BISON TRANS-
PLANTED FROM WOOD
BUFFALO NATIONAL
PARK NOW INHABIT THE
LIARD AND LOWER
NAHANNI RIVERS.

the *Nahanni Portfolio*, he tells of his grandmother and her life on the land.

> *Living in the bush was not easy. For the most part, the people lived a hand-*
> *to-mouth existence: fishing, hunting and trapping to feed and clothe them-*
> *selves. They were always on the move in search of food and game. Shelter,*
> *if any, was a stick tepee or lean-to covered with spruce bows or moose hides.*
> *Life was hard but good. It had its rewards, including a self-reliant indepen-*
> *dence and sense of freedom that may never be again.*

One does not learn intimately of spiritual matters quickly from a people who have a closely held oral tradition. What I have managed to glean by listening to Dene friends is a spiritual understanding that meshes with the world around them. The Butte plays a major role in their spiritual beliefs.

Charles Yohin, a Dene elder explained to me that Ndambadezha was a guardian of the Dene who would kill anything that was harmful to them. Long ago there had been a beaver lodge on top of Ttenago: the Butte. The beaver drowned people who were on the river by slapping his tail, creating a large wave. Ndambadezha came to the aid of the people and drove two beavers out of the lodge with a big stick. One he chased to Trout Lake to the east. The other he chased down the Mackenzie to Fort Norman. He skinned the beaver and placed it on large drying rack on the side of a mountain, and the mark remains there today.

Until the late 1800s the Dene were at odds with the Naha—the people of the mountains. The Naha were likely of Kaska descent. They dressed in Dall sheepskins and were thought to be violent. They dominated the mountainous area through which the Nahanni flows, while the Dene centred themselves along the edge of the Liard plain. From here the Dene made cautious seasonal ventures into the high country, usually in the winter to trap. In the spring they would use the moose hide craft, which Leo Norwegian had told us about as we began our journey in Fort Simpson, to navigate homeward to the Liard. By the 1880s the conflict between the Dene and Naha subsided. Perhaps the trade economy or related factors in the Yukon drew the attention of the Naha, although it is said that the Dene may finally have killed most of them. In any event the result was peace and a few Naha families settled along the Liard, liked and respected by their Dene neighbours.

Often along the shores of the Liard we spot the wood bison that have been introduced from Wood Buffalo National Park. Fortunately this group has been spared the brucellosis that plagues their cousins still in Wood Buffalo.

Finally pulling in at the Lindberg's, we were greeted by Edwin, Sue, a clutch of chickens, and a goat. Edwin was born and raised nearby. His parents Ole and Anna Lindberg are part of the history of this place. Now Edwin and Sue host river travellers in their tourist cabins. Everyone in our group used the rustic shower before a delicious supper; then we settled down for a final evening of stories around the fire.

Herb and I had made up certificates to give everyone, commemorating some comical quality they had become known for during the trip: the Shutter-Bug Award, the Jacques Cousteau Submarine License, Keeper of the Coffee. As the mood became reflective I decided to share the last entry I had made in my letter to Judy while we were floating upriver of Nahanni Butte.

> *Loitering on the current we are drifting to put off rounding the final bend*
> *that will deliver us to Nahanni Butte and our first contact with civilization.*
> *The canoes are strewn about the river, floating, detached. As I write I catch*
> *wisps of discussion, laughter and someone singing bits of Simon and*
> *Garfunkle tunes. All are the sounds of friends. I wish you could have come*
> *to know these people the way I have. Each one has brought something*
> *unique to the fibre of our little group. The Nahanni has provided the glue*
> *and as we drift out of this magical land, the "whole seems greater than the*
> *sum of the parts." As much as I look forward to seeing you again,*
> *I will miss these people.*

THE LINDBERG'S CABINS.

— *EDWIN AND SUE LINDBERG*

As I went to bed I was struck by the reality that tomorrow we would disband, shifting gears into the fast lane. Still, the Nahanni had made an impression on each of us. Sometimes I think of it as a river of youth—every time I travel it the years seem to fall away with all their petty cares and worries. Everyone seemed to be stepping more lightly that evening. I was confident that they were taking a large portion of Nahanni magic home with them. We had lived out some dreams and found some gold. Who could ask for more?

AN AFTERNOON STORM MOVES

DOWN THE VALLEY TOWARDS

SUNBLOOD MOUNTAIN.

Splash Backs

Once or twice a season we begin a trip at the Moose Ponds, the very headwaters of the Nahanni. The upper reach of the river, known as the Rock Gardens, boasts 48 kilometers of continuous whitewater. This stretch is highly regarded by experienced whitewater canoeists and is the beginning of the 170 kilometers of river lying upstream of the Nahanni Park.

Fewer paddlers attempt this portion of the river due to the technical nature of the rapids and the minimum of three weeks required to enjoy it.

THE TINY MOOSE PONDS ARE JUST LARGE ENOUGH TO LAND A FLOAT PLANE. APTLY NAMED, WE OFTEN SEE MOOSE FEEDING IN THE LAKES. A CAMP STOVE IS ESSENTIAL AS THE LAKES ARE NEAR TREE LINES. A TRAIL BEGINS ON THE WEST SHORE OF THE SECOND POND AND PROVIDES ACCESS TO THE SOUTH SLOPE OF MOUNT WILSON. A CHALLENGING SIX HOUR HIKE TO THE SUMMIT PROVIDES A PANORAMIC VIEW OF BOTH SIDES OF THE CONTINENTAL DIVIDE.

— MORTEN ASFELDT

THE 48 KILOMETERS OF CONTINUOUS CLASS 2 TO 4 WHITEWATER PROVIDE A TECHNICAL CHALLENGE FOR THE BEST CANOEISTS. SCOUTING AND LINING MAY BE REQUIRED IN PLACES. TRIPS ON THIS PORTION MUST BE PLANNED IN LATE JUNE OR JULY IN ORDER TO ENSURE ENOUGH WATER. THE MAP HIGHLIGHTS THE DETAILS. RIVER RUNNERS ARE WELL ADVISED TO OBTAIN 1:50, 000 SCALE MAPS OF THE REGION.

— CAROLE CALENSO

UPPER SOUTH NAHANNI RIVER 105 I
(MAP SHEET)

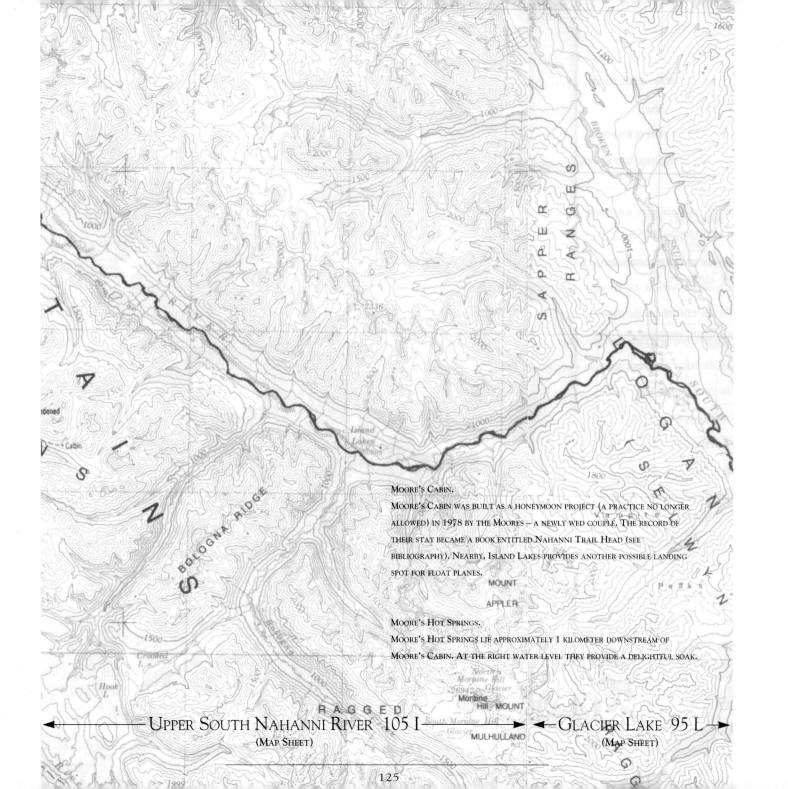

MOORE'S CABIN.

MOORE'S CABIN WAS BUILT AS A HONEYMOON PROJECT (A PRACTICE NO LONGER ALLOWED) IN 1978 BY THE MOORES – A NEWLY WED COUPLE. THE RECORD OF THEIR STAY BECAME A BOOK ENTITLED NAHANNI TRAIL HEAD (SEE BIBLIOGRAPHY). NEARBY, ISLAND LAKES PROVIDES ANOTHER POSSIBLE LANDING SPOT FOR FLOAT PLANES.

MOORE'S HOT SPRINGS.

MOORE'S HOT SPRINGS LIE APPROXIMATELY 1 KILOMETER DOWNSTREAM OF MOORE'S CABIN. AT THE RIGHT WATER LEVEL THEY PROVIDE A DELIGHTFUL SOAK.

◄— UPPER SOUTH NAHANNI RIVER 105 I —►   ◄— GLACIER LAKE 95 L —►
(MAP SHEET)   (MAP SHEET)

Taking three days or longer to hike up Brittnel Creek and into the Glacier Lake area allows you to climb into the granite Cirque of the Unclimbables amongst the highest peaks in the Northwest Territories.

—D. Salayka

FLAT RIVER 95 E
(Map Sheet)

THE LARGE EXPEDITION RAFTS USED ON THE RAFT TRIPS ALLOW FOR A TRUE "FLOAT TRIP". PADDLING IS STRICTLY
OPTIONAL AS THE GUIDE CAN MANEUVER THE CRAFT WITH THE LONG OARS.

— WOLFGANG WEBER

FIRST CANYON.

— WOLFGANG WEBER

TABLE OF ILLUSTRATIONS

TABLE OF ILLUSTRATIONS CONTINUED

Special thanks to the photographers who graciously agreed
to having their work included:

W.D. Addison

Henrick Asfeldt

Morten Asfeldt

Brad Atchison

Peter Bregg

Carole Calenso

Canadian Press

Randy Clement

Art Jones

Pat and RoseMarie Keough

Deb Ladouceur

Henry Madsen

Paul Mason

Nahanni National Park

Lisa Palechuk

Terry Palechuk

John Ross

Wendell E. White Collection

Dave Salayka

Wolfgang Weber, courtesy of the Nahanni-Ram Tourism Zone

BIBLIOGRAPHY AND SUGGESTED READING

Addison, W.D. *Nahanni National Park Historical Resources Inventory*. Parks Canada, Volume 4, A Preliminary Chronology. W.D. Addison and Associations, RR2, Kakabeka Falls, Ontario, 1976.

Berton, Pierre. *Starting Out*. McClelland and Stewart Inc., Toronto, 1987.

Berton, Pierre. *The Mysterious North*. McClelland and Stewart Inc., Toronto, 1989.

Ford, Derek. *Strange Landforms of the South Nahanni*. Canadian Geographical Journal, (February/March 1977).

Fuchs, Arved. *South Nahanni Kanu: Abenteuer Im Nordem Kanadas*. Pietsch Verlag, 1986.

Henderson, Gavin. *Heritage Saved*. An unpublished account of the movement to create Nahanni National Park.

Jowett, Peter. *Guide to the South Nahanni River*. Forthcoming.

Keough, Pat and Rosemarie. *The Nahanni Portfolio*. Stoddart, Toronto, 1988.

Mason, Bill. *Path of the Paddle*. Toronto: Van Nostrand–Reinhold, 1980.

Moor, Ronan. *Nahanni Trail Head*. Ottawa: Deneau and Greenburg, 1980.

National Geographic, September 1981.

Parks Canada 1984 Nahanni National Park Reserve, *Resource Description and Analysis*. Winnipeg: Natural Resource Conservation Section, Parks Canada, Prairie Region, 1984.

Patterson, Raymond. *The Dangerous River*. London: George Allen and Unwin Ltd., 1954; Toronto: Stoddart Publishing, 1989.

BIBLIOGRAPHY AND SUGGESTED READINGS
CONTINUED

Scotter, G.W. and J.D. Henry. *Vegetation, Wildlife and Recreational Assessment of Deadmen Valley, Nahanni National Park*. Edmonton: Canadian Wildlife Service, 1977.

Scotter, G.W., N.M. Simmons and S.C. Zoltai. *Ecology of the Nahanni and Flat River Areas: A Report to the National and Historic Parks Branch*. Edmonton: Canadian Wildlife Service, 1971.

Trudeau, Pierre E. Personal communication.

Turner, Dick. *Nahanni*. Surrey, B.C: Hancock House Publishers Ltd., 1989.

White, Wendell E. *The Birth of Nahanni: Nahanni Beguli*. Environment Canada – Parks. Microfiche Report Series.

SOURCES FOR TRAVELLERS

For information on Nahanni National Park, write to:

Nahanni National Park
Postal Bag 300, Fort Simpson, NWT, Canada X0E 0N0

Nahanni River Adventures
7603 - 109th Street, Edmonton, Alberta, Canada T6G 1C3
Tel (403) 439-1316   FAX (403) 435-3179

Canadian Recreational Canoeing Association
1029 Hyde Park Road, Ste. 5, Hyde Park, Ontario, Canada N0M 1Z0
Tel (519) 641-1261/473-2109   FAX (519) 473-6560

KANAWA MAGAZINE
For Recreational Paddling In Canada

1029 Hyde Park Road, Suite 5, Hyde Park, Ontario, Canada N0M 1Z0
Tel (519) 473-2109   FAX (519) 473-6560

• 1 year $10   • 2 years $18 (U.S.A. & Int'l add $5.00)

Canada's Canoe Adventures

1029 Hyde Park Road, Suite 5, Hyde Park, Ontario, Canada N0M 1Z0
Tel (519) 641-1261   FAX (519) 473-6560

A TANDEM CANOE IN
FIRST CANYON.

— CAROLE CALENSO

LOGS AT THE BASE OF
VIRGINIA FALLS.

— D. SALAYKA